“This isn’t my room, [illegible] **she gasped. “I asked for a standard double.’ And *that* had cost an arm and a leg.**

“You’ve clearly been upgraded,” he said silkily, drawing her into the large, luxuriously furnished sitting room, complete with a real Christmas tree dressed in festive red-and-gold decorations, before her wits could return.

When they did, she swung to face him accusingly. “This is your doing.” She glanced around wildly, as though the manager of the hotel was going to pop up like a genie out of a bottle. “I want my own room. I want the one I booked originally.”

“I understand from the receptionist that the room was snapped up minutes after I transferred to this when we arrived,” Zeke said with unforgivable satisfaction. “Look on it as your Christmas good deed. Those folks probably wouldn’t have been able to afford this penthouse, which was the only other available accommodation when I asked.”

Melody said something very rude in response, which shocked them both. And then the full significance of his words hit her. “What do you mean, ‘us’?” she bit out furiously. ‘This is my room and I’m staying in it alone—and I’ll pay for it.” Somehow.

“Payment in full has already been made,” Zeke replied, seemingly unmoved by her anger.

“Well, it can be darn well unmade.”

HELEN BROOKS was born and educated in Northampton, England. She met her husband at the age of sixteen and thirty-five years later the magic is still there. They have three lovely children and four beautiful grandchildren.

Helen began writing in 1990 as she approached that milestone of a birthday—forty! She realized that her two teenage ambitions (writing a novel and learning to drive) had been lost amid babies and family life, so she set about resurrecting them. Her first novel was accepted after one rewrite, and she passed her driving test (the former was a joy and the latter an unmitigated nightmare).

Helen is a committed Christian and fervent animal lover. She finds time is always at a premium, but somehow fits in walks in the countryside with her husband and their Irish terrier, meals out followed by the cinema or theater, reading, swimming and visiting with friends. She also enjoys sitting in her wonderfully therapeutic, rambling old garden in the sun with a glass of red wine (under the guise of resting while thinking, of course!).

Since becoming a full-time writer, Helen has found her occupation to be one of pure joy. She loves exploring what makes people tick and finds the old adage "truth is stranger than fiction" to be absolutely true. She would love to hear from any readers, care of Harlequin Presents®.

Books by Helen Brooks

Harlequin Presents® Extra

113—SWEET SURRENDER WITH THE MILLIONAIRE
130—SNOWBOUND SEDUCTION

Other titles by this author available in eBook

A Christmas Night
to Remember
HELEN BROOKS

~ One Christmas Night In... ~

TORONTO NEW YORK LONDON
AMSTERDAM PARIS SYDNEY HAMBURG
STOCKHOLM ATHENS TOKYO MILAN MADRID
PRAGUE WARSAW BUDAPEST AUCKLAND

Recycling programs
for this product may
not exist in your area.

ISBN-13: 978-0-373-52842-4

A CHRISTMAS NIGHT TO REMEMBER

First North American Publication 2011

A CHRISTMAS
NIGHT TO REMEMBER

CHAPTER ONE

How could you have longed for something with all your heart, lived through endless minutes and hours and days and weeks anticipating the moment it happened, and be numbingly terrified now it had?

Melody shut her eyes tightly, wrinkling her face as she told herself to get control. She could do this. She had to do it actually. There wasn't a choice. By tonight her hospital bed could be occupied by someone else, and topping and tailing was strictly against the rules.

The brief moment of dark humour helped to restore her equilibrium. She slowly unclenched her hands, which had been fists at her sides, and opened her eyes. The small room—one of four off the main ward—had been home for three months since the accident. Early on one of the nurses attending her had told her it was mostly long-term patients who were placed in the more private *en-suite* rooms. She suspected Sarah, the nurse in question, had been trying to warn her not to expect miracles. The damage she'd done to her spine and legs when she'd stepped in front of a lorry one morning wasn't going to be a quick fix. As it happened she hadn't needed it spelling out. She'd known she'd changed her life for ever when she'd looked into Zeke's contorted face as she'd emerged from the fog of anaesthetic after the initial emergency operation.

Enough. Don't think of him. You need to be strong this morning.

Obeying the inner voice, Melody reached for her thick, warmly insulated jacket. In spite of the hospital's hot-house central heating, she knew it was freezing outside. The experts had been predicting a white Christmas for days, and it seemed they were going to be right for once. There had already been an odd flurry of snow this morning, and the sky was low over the rooftops beyond the hospital precincts.

Melody walked across to the window and gazed at the view she would be seeing for the last time. The car park was busy—it was always busy—and beyond the walled grounds the streets of London stretched away full of houses and offices and industry and people going about their everyday business. Normal people. She bit hard on her inner lip. Girls who wouldn't have to think twice about wearing a short skirt in the summer or a bikini. She had been like that once. Now every advertisement on TV and every magazine she read seemed full of perfect women, girls with long beautiful legs and flawless skin.

Enough. She turned from the window, hating herself for the self-pity which always seemed to hit when she least expected it. She was lucky to be alive, she knew that, and she was grateful for it. The damage to her spine and mangled legs, not least the huge amount of blood she'd lost at the scene of the accident, had meant it was touch-and-go for days, apparently, although she hadn't known much about it. She had vague memories of Zeke sitting by her bed, holding her hand in Intensive

Care, but it had been a full week before she had woken one morning and found her mind was her own again.

That all seemed like a long time ago now. As soon as she could be moved from the hospital in Reading she'd been transferred to this one, which specialised in spinal injuries. She hadn't known Zeke had been instrumental in accomplishing this, or that with her type of injuries expert care was essential for good long-term recovery until recently, when her consultant had mentioned it. Not that it would have made any difference to her decision to end their marriage.

Melody limped across to the narrow bed, staring down at the suitcase she had packed earlier that morning. She had all the relevant documentation and had said her goodbyes. It only remained for her to leave the place which had become comfortingly womb-like in its safety over the past weeks and months, even as she'd longed to be in charge of her own life once again. But here it didn't matter that she walked with an ungainly gait. The nursing staff were so proud of her that she'd fought to walk at all. They didn't wince at the sight of her scars, but praised her for the way she'd tackled the painful physiotherapy day after exhausting day.

Outside the walls of the hospital was the real world. Zeke's world. She swallowed hard. A realm where the rich and beautiful had the power, and nothing less than perfection would do. She had inhabited that world once—briefly.

She straightened her shoulders, telling herself such thoughts would only weaken her when she needed to be strong, but somehow today she found she couldn't control her mind the way she had done since she'd told Zeke their marriage was over and she didn't want him to visit her again.

Zeke James—entrepreneur extraordinaire, king of the show-business world he ruled with ruthless detachment. She had heard of him long before she'd met him while auditioning as a dancer for a new show. Everyone in the show-business world had heard of Zeke. He was the living embodiment of a man with the Midas touch.

She had arrived late for the audition—an absolute no-no if you were serious about a job. For every dancer selected there was likely to be over a hundred or more who were disappointed—competition was fierce and jobs were scarce. But old Mrs. Wood, the elderly widow who had occupied the ground-floor bedsit of the house she'd been living in, had found her beloved cat dead in the road first thing that morning, and had been so upset she hadn't felt able to leave her until the frail little woman's married daughter had arrived. Consequently she had raced into the theatre where the auditions were being held breathless and red-faced, and had been given a dressing-down by the dance director in front of everyone without being allowed to say why she was late. By the time she had ventured onto the stage to dance her piece she had given up all hope of gaining a place in the chorus line, much less that of lead female dancer which was what she'd applied for.

Perhaps that was why she had performed the routine she'd practised every evening so perfectly—she'd had nothing to lose. She had felt as if her body was a musical instrument, tuned and played as finely as a violin, and she'd responded to the piano, any nerves melting away as she'd flowed with the rhythm, her timing faultless.

Melody's mouth trembled for a second. Never again would she feel like that. One momentary loss of concentration and the career she had worked so hard for had been smashed for ever. All the training since she had been a child, the sacrifices, the time spent pushing her body to reach levels of physical fitness and agility greater than that needed by most top athletes had been for nothing. The years dancing in clubs and pantomime and cabaret as she'd honed her craft, the waitressing and bar work she'd done to pay the rent between engagements, the lack of opportunity to put down any roots since most dance companies undertook tours both at home and abroad, the poor pay and constant discipline—all pointless now.

But none of that mattered as much as losing Zeke.

Melody continued to stand staring into the compact little room but she was miles away, lost in memories.

The first time she had seen Zeke was when she had finished the audition and someone had risen from the small group sitting in the auditorium and begun to clap slowly. She'd stood, panting slightly and unsure how to respond, and her gaze had focused on a tall, broad-shouldered man with dark hair and rugged features.

'Excellent, Miss…' he had consulted the notes in his hand '…Miss Brown. Better late than never. Or do we have a prima donna on our hands who expects us to be grateful that she bothered to turn up at all?'

She had instinctively known he was Zeke James; everyone backstage had been buzzing with the fact the great man himself was present. She had also disliked him on the spot. She detested sarcasm, and the deep, faintly husky voice had been oozing with it. Drawing herself up to her full five-foot-ten-inches—something which had spoilt her chances of becoming a successful ballet dancer but which hadn't interfered with her career as a modern stage dancer—she'd tried to keep her voice from betraying her when she said, 'I'm sorry I was late but it was unavoidable.'

'Really?' he'd drawled. 'I would like to know what came before a place in my production, Miss Brown? I presume it was nothing less than a life-or-death matter?'

'Death, actually.'

She could see she'd taken him aback—whether because of the hostile note she'd failed to keep hidden or the content of her reply she wasn't sure; whatever, it had been immensely satisfying to see him at a loss for a moment, even if she knew she'd just blown the faintest chance which had remained of being offered a job.

He'd recovered almost immediately, of course. 'I'm sorry.' His eyes had narrowed as he'd stared at her more intently before sitting down once more.

Once in the wings, a couple of the other dancers she knew had gathered round her and she'd filled them in on what had happened as they all waited to find out their fate.

'A cat?' Katie, a tall redhead who was easily the most ambitious person Melody had ever met, had stared at her in disbelief. 'When we heard you say a death we thought it must be your nearest and dearest to stop you trying for the part of Sasha, but it was just a *cat*?'

'It might be just a cat to you, but it was Mrs Wood's companion and best friend and she was heartbroken this morning,' she'd answered, knowing even as she spoke Katie would never understand. Like acting, dancing was highly competitive, and only about one in ten dancers registered with Equity was in work at any one time. Prospects were always poor. Every dance teacher she'd ever had had hammered home the fact that it was only the most dedicated and talented dancers who succeeded, and if you had a thick skin and were ruthless to boot it was all to the good.

Katie, who was also trying for the lead female dancer's role, had unwittingly confirmed her thoughts when she'd said, 'Darling, you're a sweetie, you really are, but I wouldn't have kept Zeke James waiting if my dear old mother had kicked the bucket in front of my very eyes this morning. You have to look after number one in this world because no one else will, take it from me. It's dog eat dog.'

One of the other dancers had chipped in at this point. 'And we all know you'd step on any one of us, Katie, if it gave you an edge in getting what you want, never mind an old lady and her cat.'

'Too true.' Katie had grinned, completely unabashed. 'And the only difference between me and you is that I admit it up front. You'd do the same, Sue. And you, Christie. We all would except perhaps Melody, our own little angel of mercy.'

It was only at this point that they had become aware of Zeke James, the dance director and the producer standing having a cup of coffee some distance away. That the three men must have been able to hear their conversation became apparent when Zeke strolled over a few moments later, his face deadpan as he murmured softly, so no one else could overhear, 'It's the first time I've played second fiddle to a cat, Miss Brown. A novel experience.'

He had walked on before she could retaliate, and when she had glanced over at Katie something in the other girl's face had made her suspect Katie had known Zeke James and the others were within earshot all the time.

Ten minutes later they were all called back on stage.

She had got the part of Sasha and Katie was her understudy. And when she had left the theatre later that day Zeke's black Ferrari had been waiting for her…

Enough. Melody shook her head, forcing the memories back into the little box in her mind where they remained under lock and key most of the time. Today, though, she didn't seem able to prevent them escaping.

Flicking her silky, shoulder-length strawberry-blond hair—which just missed being Titian—free from the collar of her coat, Melody reached for her suitcase. Her hands were trembling. Taking several deep breaths, she composed herself, and when she studied them again they were steady. A small victory, but heartening.

She was going to be fine. She nodded to the thought. Her plans had been carefully made. All she had to do was take it a day at a time now. The hospital thought she was going to stay with friends, but once she'd known she could leave the day before Christmas Eve she had phoned numerous London hotels until she'd found a room, reserving it for a full week. Due to a mix-up with her paperwork her departure had been delayed for a day, but the hotel had kept her room when she'd let them know she would now be arriving on Christmas Eve instead. The room had been expensive, but with it being the holiday period she'd been lucky to find one at all. It would give her the breathing space she needed and that was all that mattered. She nodded again.

Once in the main ward Melody was touched by how the nursing staff gathered round, despite her having said her goodbyes earlier that morning, but then at last she was free to leave and make her way to the lifts. She hadn't expected to feel so shaky and overcome, and as the lift sped her downwards to the hospital lobby it was as though she was venturing into hostile alien territory.

When it stopped and the doors slid silently open she had to force herself to move.

A large robust man brushed past her on his way to the lift, and although the action was slight it was enough to knock her off balance due to her injuries. Melody stumbled, the weight of her bulging case hampering her regaining control, and to her horror she knew she was going to fall. She had firmly resisted all suggestions of a stick or crutches, but walking the length of the ward and pacing her room was very different from negotiating a crowded hospital foyer.

And then suddenly a pair of strong arms was holding her, steadying her, and the next moment the suitcase was taken out of her hand.

'Hello, Melody.' Zeke's voice was expressionless, his ebony eyes unreadable as they stared down into her startled green ones.

'What—?' She was so surprised her brain wouldn't compute. 'How—?'

'Questions later.' He was leading her towards the huge automatic doors with a firm hand at her elbow and she had no choice but to walk with him. 'For now let's get out of here.'

CHAPTER TWO

IT was the impact of the freezing air outside the hot-house warmth of the hospital that jolted her out of her shock. Her wits returning along with her voice, Melody jerked her arm free, stopping dead as she faced him. 'What are you doing here?' she bit out hotly.

'Isn't it obvious? Collecting my wife.'

His voice was unruffled, even lazy, but Melody knew better than to be fooled that was how he was feeling inside. Zeke was a master at disguising his thoughts and emotions; it was one of the attributes which had made him so hugely successful.

There were plenty more.

At thirty-eight years of age, Zeke had been building his empire for twenty years with a ruthless determination devoid of sentiment. He was no respecter of persons; in the two years since they had been married—she had walked down the aisle on her twenty-fifth birthday—Melody had come to realise that, whether someone was a big star or a virtual novice, Zeke treated each artist exactly the same. He expected total dedication and one-hundred-per-cent commitment and if he got that he was charm itself. If he didn't...

Undoubtedly the charisma he exuded as naturally as breathing helped—especially with the ladies. He was

tall at six-foot-four and big with it, although Melody
knew for a fact there wasn't an inch of surplus fat on
the muscled male body. His broad shoulders and tough
physique dwarfed most other men, and his face was
hard and rough-hewn, too strong-featured to be called
handsome by any stretch of the imagination. But he had
something much more powerful than pretty-boy good-
looks: a magnetism that emphasised his raw masculinity and cynical, sexy appeal.

The sharply defined planes and angles of his face
were unsoftened by his jet-black hair and dark ebony
eyes framed by thick short lashes, but it was his mouth
which had always fascinated her. In repose it was deliciously uneven and stomach-quiveringly attractive, and
his voice... On their first date she had felt she could
listen to the deep, smoky tones for ever. She still did.

But she had made her decision and it was irrevocable.
She didn't belong in Zeke's world any more. Perhaps
she never had. And she wasn't going to cling onto him
until even the memories of the happiest time in her life
were soured by the present. She had never understood
what it was about her that had made him love her in the
first place—not when he could have had any woman he
liked—but the Melody he had married was gone.

Forcing a strength into her voice that belied her trembling inside, Melody said, 'How did you know I was
leaving today? I haven't told anyone.'

'But I'm not anyone. I am your husband.' He smiled,
but it didn't reach the coal-black eyes.

A sliver of ice ran down her spine. She recognised
that smile that wasn't a smile, although it had never been
directed at her before. But then she had never had occasion to challenge him in the past and come up against

his inflexible will. 'We're separated and I've told you I want a divorce.'

'And I've told you only over my dead body,' he said conversationally. 'So, do we stand here in the cold, discussing this for the next umpteen minutes, or are you going to be sensible and come home with me?'

Now she felt a welcome flood of adrenaline as her temper rose. 'I have no intention of doing either.' She glanced over at the taxi rank outside the hospital gates. 'I'm getting a cab to where I want to go, so may I have my case, please?'

He shook his head. 'No can do.'

She glared at him. 'I mean it, Zeke.'

'So do I.'

'Fine. Keep it.' She had her handbag over her shoulder, containing her credit cards and cash. 'But just leave me alone.'

'Stop this.' The studiously calm pose vanished. 'I've stayed away the last six weeks, as you asked. I thought that would give you time to come to your senses after the doctor said my presence was upsetting you and hindering your recovery—' the icy quality to his words told her how he had received that news '—but I'm damned if this ridiculous farce is continuing for another hour. You're my wife—we're in this for the long haul, remember? For richer or poorer, in sickness or health, till death do us part.'

She only heard the 'long haul' part. It suggested gritted teeth, a fulfilment of duty, doing the 'right thing' when everything in him was crying out against it. It confirmed all her fears. She felt herself shrinking, dwindling away to nothing.

Zeke had never made any secret of the fact that he delighted in her body. Every night of their marriage and sometimes in the day too he had worshiped her with his lovemaking, taking her to heights she had never imagined as they gloried in each other. He was a skilful and generous lover, adventurous but infinitely tender, intent always on giving her pleasure even as he satisfied his own desire. She had never slept with anyone before Zeke because she had never been in love with any of the men she had dated, and she'd always known she wanted to wait for 'the one'. And then Zeke had blazed into her life like a dark, glittering meteor, and within two months of their first meeting she had been Mrs James.

Melody took a deep breath, and as she did so the first starry snowflake wafted by in the wind. 'It takes two to keep a marriage together, Zeke. You can't force me to stay.'

'I don't believe I'm hearing this.'

'Believe it because I mean every word.' She was amazed her poise was holding. 'Things are different now.'

His opinion of her last statement was decidedly profane, but she didn't flinch in the face of his anger. He stared at her after his outburst, conflict evident in every line and contour of his rugged features. 'Are you telling me you don't love me any more?' he ground out finally. 'Is that it?'

She lowered her eyes from the brilliant black orbs boring into her. She couldn't lie convincingly otherwise. Allowing her hair to swing forward and hide her face, she muttered, 'Yes, that's it. I don't love you. All right?'

'Look at me and say it.' His fingers forced her chin upwards. 'Tell me you're prepared to wipe away the last couple of years and all we've shared together as though they never happened. Tell me that and look me in the face while you do it.'

'Of course they happened, and I'll always be grateful for them, but things move on. People change.' She could hear herself saying the words as though it was someone else speaking.

'I haven't changed!' He suddenly shook his head in rapid movement, signifying a silent apology for his raised voice. 'I haven't changed,' he repeated more softly, the sensual, smoky quality to his voice apparent. 'And I simply don't believe you have either.'

'Oh, I have,' she said, with such bitterness he couldn't fail to believe her. He had married a young, whole woman. Now she didn't feel young any more and she certainly wasn't whole. She was a mess, inside and out. And there was no room in Zeke's world for emotional and physical cripples.

'You mean the accident? Your legs?' He was speaking so quietly she almost couldn't hear him. 'That doesn't make any difference to me—surely you know that? You're still you—'

'No.' Her voice was brittle but with a thread of steel running through it. 'I'm different, Zeke. And you can't wave a magic wand and make me the old Melody, any more than you can pretend I'm not damaged. I'll never dance again. I'll never even walk without a limp. I have months of intensive physiotherapy in front of me and they've already warned me the chances of arthritis as I get older are high. I could end up in a wheelchair at worst.'

'I know all that. I've been seeing the consultant on a regular basis and I have worked out a programme of treatment with him.' Before she could react, he took her arm again, adding, 'It's starting to snow and you're getting cold. Come and sit in the car at least.'

'I've told you I'm getting a cab.' He was wearing a black overcoat and he looked very big and dark as he glanced down at her. A part of her noticed the way his hair curled over his collar, unlike his usual short, almost military style. Was that intended or did he need a haircut? For some reason she found the thought weakening, and to combat this her voice had a sharp edge as she added, 'And I don't want you talking to my consultant again, okay? Much less deciding on my treatment. I can look after myself. We're not together any more, Zeke. Deal with it.'

Before she had met Zeke she had looked after herself for years after all. She knew from her grandmother that her father had walked out on her mother before she was born, but, her mother having died when Melody was little more than a baby, she had no recollection of her. Her maternal grandmother had brought her up, and as her mother had been an only child there had been no aunts and uncles or cousins in her life, and her grandfather had divorced her grandmother years earlier and moved away.

Consequently it had been a somewhat singular childhood, especially as her grandmother had discouraged friendships with other children. She had lived for the twice-weekly dance lessons she'd attended since a small child. At the age of sixteen she'd been accepted at a dance school and had just graduated from there when her grandmother had passed away, leaving her a small inheritance. She had moved from her home town in the west of England to the capital, finding a bedsit and beginning to look for dancing work while practising every day. Once her nest egg was gone she'd been forced to take other jobs between dancing engagements to pay the bills, but she had been happy enough while she waited for her 'big break'. And then the part of Sasha had come along and she had met Zeke and her life had changed for ever.

'You're being extremely childish, Melody,' Zeke said, in a tone which one would use with a recalcitrant toddler having a tantrum. 'At least let me drive you to where you want to go. What do you think I'm going to do, for crying out loud? Kidnap you and spirit you away against your will?'

It was exactly the kind of thing he *would* do, and her face was answer enough. Her green eyes were a perfect mirror of her thoughts.

Zeke clicked his tongue in exasperation. 'I give you my word—how's that? But you must see we need to talk? You owe me that at least. The last time we talked you were all but hysterical and I had half the medical team at the hospital breathing down my neck and accusing me of delaying your recovery. I didn't understand what I'd done wrong then and I still don't. And I intend to get to the bottom of this.'

'I wrote to you last week,' she said flatly, knowing he had a point. But how could she explain to Zeke what she didn't fully understand herself? She just knew it was impossible for them to be together. 'There's nothing more to be said.'

'Ah, yes, a lovely little missive,' Zeke said with heavy sarcasm. 'A few lines stating you wanted a divorce, that you required nothing at all in the way of settlement and that in view of this kindness you expected the divorce to go through without contest. Well, I've got news for you. There's no way—*no way*—I'm going to let you walk away from me. You're my wife. When I made those vows they were for life. It wasn't some kind of nice little event that could be put to one side when it suited.'

Her chin came up. 'I'm not a possession, Zeke, like your Ferrari or your villa in Madeira. This acquisition can think and feel.'

'Don't twist my words,' he said with remarkable calm. 'Now, are you going to let me take you where you're going without a scene or shall I put you over my shoulder and carry you to the car? The choice is yours. I'm easy either way.'

She didn't make the mistake of saying *You wouldn't dare.* Zeke would dare. Drawing on what was left of her limited supply of dignity, she eyed him icily before allowing him to lead her in the direction of the car. It wasn't hard to pick it out. There weren't too many sleek black Ferraris crouching in the hospital grounds. The car was like its master—distinctive.

The few desultory flakes of a minute ago were thickening into a real snowstorm as Zeke helped her into the car. She watched him as he walked round the bonnet, her heart aching and her stomach churning. This was just the sort of confrontation she'd been hoping to avoid, but then she might have known Zeke wouldn't give up so easily. She *had* known it. Hoped, even? a little voice asked. Which was ridiculous and self-indulgent. Zeke was constantly surrounded by the cream of the entertainment industry, and it wasn't just the wannabes who offered themselves to him on a plate. Women were drawn to him like pins to a magnet. She had seen it so often at parties and functions. He had that undefinable something which would be worth a fortune if it could be bottled and which had nothing to do with his wealth. She'd often teased him and said he'd have made an irresistible gigolo if he'd decided on a different career. It didn't seem so funny now. Then she had been confident in her youth and perfectly honed body. Now...

He didn't start the car immediately, turning to her in the luxurious leather-clad interior as he slid an arm along the back of her seat. 'I've missed you,' he said huskily, the ebony eyes as soft as black velvet. 'Every minute, every hour.'

No, don't do this. His anger and irritation she could cope with; then he was the Zeke the world knew—hard, determined, ruthless. But with her he had always been the opposite to those things. And when a man as big and masculine as Zeke revealed his soft centre it was terribly seductive. From the first evening, when he had waited for her outside the theatre, he had been open and vulnerable with her in a way that had cut through her initial dislike and antagonism like a knife through butter. The more so when she had learnt his history.

Zeke had grown up in the care system from the age of eight, when his single mother had finally abandoned him after years of neglect and disappeared who knew where. He freely admitted to having been a troublesome child and an even more troublesome youth, and remembered one teacher predicting he'd either be a villain or a millionaire—or maybe both—by the time he was thirty after yet another of his misdeeds had come to light.

'That teacher did me a favour, although he didn't know it at the time,' Zeke had told her one evening over dinner at a fancy restaurant, when she'd been seeing him for a couple of weeks. 'It was one of those crossroads in life—a decision time, you know? It would have been easy to go down the dark route—I was already more than halfway there—but to make a fortune legitimately was harder. More of a challenge. And I've always liked a challenge. So I decided to prove something to him and to myself.'

She remembered she had stared at him, fascinated. 'And is that the only reason you veered on the side of law and order?'

'I should say no—that deep down I wanted to do the right and noble thing—shouldn't I?' he'd answered with the crooked grin which had already become so familiar to her. 'But the truth of it is I didn't think that way then. I'd lived in dumps mixing with all kinds of types when I was with my mother, and once in care I developed a huge chip on my shoulder. I was an angry young man, I guess.' His grin had widened. 'I'd have been an excellent villain, though.'

She'd laughed with him. 'I'm glad you chose the route you did,' she'd said a little breathlessly, somewhat overwhelmed.

His face had straightened and he'd reached across the table for her hand. 'So am I,' he said softly, 'and never more than at this moment. I would have found it very hard to look into your eyes and ask you to love a man like that.'

She'd blinked before murmuring, 'And is that what you're asking me to do? To fall in love with you?'

'I've loved you from the minute you stood on that stage and put me in my place, and I've never told another woman I love her because it hasn't been true before. I don't want to rush you but I want to marry you, Melody. I want you to be my wife, the mother of my children, my partner through life. I love you, I want you, I need you and I adore you.' He'd let go of her hand and leant back in his seat. 'Does that answer your question?' he'd drawled self-mockingly.

They had got engaged that night and married six weeks later, and she had felt her life had only begun the day she had met Zeke. To have someone who was hers, who loved her, had been sweet.

She turned her head from him now, hardening her voice as she said, 'You shouldn't have come here today, Zeke.'

'The hell I shouldn't. Nothing could have prevented me.'

The snow was coating the windscreen in a blanket of white, shutting them in their own little world. He was so close the faint familiar smell of his aftershave mingled with leather from the car's interior, evoking memories Melody could have done without. Memories that turned her fluid inside.

She knew he was going to kiss her, and when he turned her chin to face him she didn't resist, steeling herself instead to show no reaction as his mouth claimed hers. It was a slow, leisurely, sensual kiss, not the hard, possessive onslaught she'd half been expecting, and it took all her willpower not to respond to the magic of his lips. But she managed it. Just.

When his mouth lifted from hers she saw his eyes were narrowed as he searched her face. 'I see,' he murmured after a moment. 'Do you think you can keep it up?'

His body warmth reached out to her, dark and compelling, as she swallowed hard before muttering, 'I don't know what you mean.'

He smiled faintly. 'Of course you don't.' He leaned forward again and kissed her thoroughly and with an enjoyment he made no effort to rein in, and by the time he finished Melody was not only kissing him back but trembling with desire.

'There.' His voice was very soft as he tilted his head to look down into the clear green of her eyes. 'That's better.' He stroked a strand of blond hair from her cheek, his touch tender. 'Can we go home now?'

Melody stared into the tough, furrowed face and suddenly a flood of anger burnt up all other emotion. Drawing away from him, she said bitingly, 'Is that all you think it takes? A kiss and I'm putty in your hands?'

A muscle in his cheek twitched at her direct hit.

'I'm not going home with you, Zeke. Not today, not tomorrow, not any time.' Ignoring the cloud of fury darkening his features, she continued, 'Whether you accept it or not, our marriage is over. Now, if you're not going to take me to the hotel I've booked into, I'll get there under my own steam. Okay?'

There was a long pause when he turned from her and gripped the steering wheel as though he wanted to break it. Then without a word he started the engine and the powerful car growled into life. 'Where do you want to go?' he asked coldly, his tone searing her, and after she'd given the name and street of the hotel he pulled out of the parking space.

She had won. He'd given in. As they passed through the hospital gates she sat still and numb, refusing to feel or let herself think. The time for that could come later, when she was alone. For now she had to remain in the bubble that had surrounded her. It was the only way to retain her sanity.

CHAPTER THREE

MELODY hadn't seen a photograph of the hotel; with most of the ones she had tried being full for Christmas it had been a case of beggars couldn't be choosers. Now, as Zeke pulled up in front of the somewhat shabby exterior of the building situated in a side street off the Bayswater Road, Melody took a deep breath. 'I'm sorry,' she said painfully, 'I really am. But one day you'll see this was for the best. Thank you for meeting me today but I think it's better if we communicate only through our solicitors from now on.'

Zeke said nothing, exiting the car and walking round the bonnet to help her out, his dark face grim.

It was a less than elegant emergence onto the pavement due to her damaged legs and as unlike her normal natural poise as was possible to imagine. Knowing Zeke's appreciation of grace and style, Melody cringed inside, before telling herself it was all to the good. This was reality, and if he was repulsed by her clumsiness it only underlined the sense of what she had been saying: that they had no possible future together.

She glanced at his face as he shut the passenger door, but the inscrutable features could have been set in stone and revealed nothing. When he extracted her case she reached out a hand for it but he ignored the action, taking her arm as he steered her towards the hotel's glass doors.

Once inside the lobby—which wasn't half as bad as she'd expected from the exterior of the building—she said firmly, 'Thank you,' as she extended a hand for the case once more. 'I can take it from here.'

'Sit down.' He deposited her on one of the plump sofas the lobby held as he spoke. 'I'll check you in and get the case sent to your room and then we're going to lunch. Is there anything in the case you need before it disappears?'

Melody shook her head. Her medication was in her handbag. 'But I don't think—'

'Good. Don't think,' he said with grim sarcasm. 'For once in your life just listen.'

She stared at his back as he walked over to the reception desk and muttered several words under her breath. Her head was spinning, her legs were hurting and her back was aching like mad. When she'd been cocooned in her little room at the hospital her proposed plans for this momentous day—her emergence into the big bad world once more—had seemed straightforward. The doctors had warned her it would be tiring after the weeks spent in bed or sitting in the chair in her room, and she had imagined taking a cab here and then retiring for most of the day and using Room Service if she wanted anything to eat. She hadn't expected to feel quite so weak and wiped out, though, but perhaps that was due more to seeing Zeke than her physical condition.

He was back in a couple of minutes. 'All taken care of,' he said with annoying satisfaction, 'and they're serving lunch in the restaurant in an hour so I've asked the concierge to park the car. They have a few spaces reserved for staff but they were very helpful. Very help-ful indeed.'

She didn't doubt it. Money had a way of smoothing out such issues and Zeke was always generous.

'I thought you'd prefer to eat here than elsewhere,' he continued, sitting down beside her. 'You look tired. And I've ordered coffee while we wait.'

Melody felt herself bristling. How dared he take over like this, and what did he mean by saying she looked tired? That she looked haggard and unattractive? Well, she didn't need him to tell her that. Her mirror did a perfect job every morning. She hadn't slept well since the accident and when she did nod off her dreams were mostly nightmares.

After glaring at him she turned to look out of the window next to the sofa. Big fat flakes of snow were settling on the ground and already rooftops were cov-ered with a glistening mantle. It was going to be a white Christmas for sure. Last year they had spent the holiday skiing in Switzerland, returning to their wonderful little lodge each night and spending the evenings wrapped in each other's arms in front of the blazing log fire drink-ing hot toddies. She had been due to be involved in a big production in the West End in the New Year, likely to run for a good while, and life had been sweet. They had talked about having a family one day, of course, but not for years. Most dancers had to finish their ca-reer in their mid-thirties and Zeke had been content to wait until she was ready.

As though he could read her mind, he said quietly, 'Looks like we wouldn't have to chase the snow this year like last. It's come to us instead.'

'Except there's not much skiing down the Bayswater Road,' she said as lightly as she could, knowing her days of such sports were over. 'Not unless you want to be taken away by men in white coats.'

Zeke chuckled, and then almost immediately his smile died and he leant forward. 'Talk to me, Dee,' he urged, unconsciously using his own private nickname for her. 'Tell me how you feel, what this is really about. I need to know—you can surely see that? This excuse about not feeling the same isn't you.'

It *was* the truth and it wasn't. And deep down she had known she would have to explain herself fully for Zeke to accept they were finished. She had hoped by shutting him out and refusing to let him visit her in hospital his resentment and manly pride would overshadow his feelings for her, but Zeke wasn't so shallow as that. At the same time she knew how he felt about sickness. In the years with his mother, before she had left, he'd been brought up in the most squalid of surroundings, often rubbing shoulders with drug addicts and down-and-outs, meths drinkers and the like. It had left him with an almost pathological resolve to take care of his own body and he couldn't understand people who were careless about their health. Her perfectly honed, supple dancer's body and extreme physical fitness had formed a large part of her attraction for him; she knew that although he had never spelt it out in so many words. And now...

Choosing her words carefully, she looked him full in the face. 'Zeke, will you listen to me? *Really* listen and not interrupt until I've finished? Will you do that?'

He nodded, his face tense. 'If you tell me the truth.'

'You asked me earlier if I still love you and the answer to that is of course I do.' At his sudden movement she held up her hand, palm facing him. 'You promised,' she reminded him.

He settled back, his ebony eyes intent on hers. 'Go on.'

'But now, after the accident, my loving you or you loving me is not enough. From a little girl all I've ever wanted to do was dance. It was my life. I was totally dedicated to and disciplined by the demands of ballet up until I grew too tall, but as long as I could carry on dancing I didn't mind too much. You know how fierce the competition is within the entertainment business, but it never caused me a moment's doubt because I *had* to dance. It was as simple as that. And now that is over.'

The waiter arriving with coffee interrupted her, and Melody waited until he had bustled off before she went on. 'I know I could have been killed that day, and I am grateful to be alive, but I can never go back to the way things were. I'm all at sea at the moment, I admit it, but one thing I do know is that if I don't want to drown in a sludge of self-pity I have to make a new life for myself far away from the world I've embraced for the last decade. And Zeke...' She paused, not knowing how to say it but then deciding there were no right words. 'You're the embodiment of that world. You love it; it's food and drink to you; it's your whole life.'

He again made a movement to speak and was stopped by her raised hand. 'But that's only part of why I have to leave. You're surrounded by women who see you as the means of their getting on in the business. Beautiful women—talented, young, ambitious—and we've laughed in the past at what some of them will do to get your attention. I've been there when you've been blatantly propositioned. I know how far some of them will go. I didn't like it then and I like it still less now.'

She was trembling and took a sip of her coffee, needing the caffeine. The next part was harder to say.

'Then I could be everything you need. Now I can't. We have to be honest here, to face facts. You have a crippled wife. You—the head of the entertainment business. When we would attend functions and dinners and walk the red carpet and so on I'd be hobbling along beside you. There might even come a day when you'd be pushing me in a wheelchair. Or I'd stay at home, watching from afar, wondering which starlet was trying her luck that night. I'd turn into someone I don't want to be and in turn you'd change. I don't want us to end like that. Far better a clean break now, while we still care about each other and have good memories to look back on.'

He was staring at her as though she were mad, and now nothing could have stopped his next words. 'This is rubbish—absolute rubbish,' he bit out with controlled fury. 'This isn't you and me you're talking about here. What we have is stronger and better than the people you've painted. And these supposedly beautiful women you've gone on about—what are you if not beautiful? Inside and out?'

'But I'm not, Zeke, not any more.' She was as white as the snow outside the window but determined to make him see. 'I have scars—angry, red, puckered things that are gouged into the skin you used to say was like honey-coloured silk—and they'll always be there. Oh, they might fade some, but they'll still be ugly until the day I die. This isn't going to go away.'

'I don't care about your scars. Only inasmuch as they affect your perception of yourself,' he added softly.

'You haven't seen them.' She stared at him, dying inside.

'And whose fault is that? When I asked to see them you went hysterical and I was thrown out of your room and warned not to mention it again. You'd show me when you were ready, they said. But the next thing I know I'm warned visiting you at all is doing you more harm than good and if I care about you I have to give you a breathing space. Well if the "breathing space" resulted in these damn fool ideas you've got I should have carried on visiting. I love *you*, dammit—every part of you, scars and all—and I resent being labelled as some pathetic bozo who will bed any women on offer. That's not who I am and you know it.'

Two spots of colour burnt in her ashen face now as her own temper rose. 'I didn't say that.'

'That's exactly what you said.' He was breathing hard and still furiously angry. 'Okay, let me ask you something. What if it had been me in that accident? What if I'd been the one having the operations and months in hospital? What if it was my legs? Would you be looking around for someone else?'

'Of course I wouldn't. You know I wouldn't.'

'Then why the hell do you think I would? And what makes your love so damn superior to mine? Because that's what you're insinuating, however you dress it up, and I resent that.'

'You're twisting my words,' she said helplessly, on the verge of tears. 'I never said my love is better than yours.'

Zeke looked at her trembling lips, at the bruised blue shadows under her eyes from where she hadn't slept and her too-slim frame where the weight had dropped off her. Swearing softly, he pulled her into him, careless of where they were. 'Don't cry,' he muttered thickly. 'I don't want to make you cry. I want to love you and care for you and make it all better, but you're driving me mad, woman. Stark, staring mad. I've nearly gone insane the last few weeks. I even resorted to coming to the hospital at night and sitting outside in the car park just to be near you. Crazy, eh? But that's how it's been.'

Melody relaxed against him for a moment—but only a moment. Far from reassuring her, his words had hammered home the fact that Zeke wasn't seeing things clearly. He couldn't make it all better—no one could—and the words he'd spoken earlier, about being in it for the long haul, were at the forefront of her mind. He felt staying with her, supporting her, protecting her, was his duty. And duty wasn't a bad thing, even if there were folk these days who regarded it as a four-letter word; she just didn't want it to be the reason for their marriage to continue. She couldn't live with pity. His pity.

Drawing away from him, she made herself finish her cup of coffee. After a moment or two he did the same, but the ebony eyes remained fixed on her delicate features as he drank. 'This is partly to do with your grandmother,' he said after a little while. 'You know that, don't you? A damn big part too.'

Caught unawares, she shot her gaze to meet his. 'What on earth are you talking about? My grandmother has been dead for years.'

'I know she brought you up and you loved her,' he said tersely, 'but she wasn't exactly a fan of the male of the species, from what you've told me. She never let you forget that your father walked out on your mother, and your grandfather's affairs were mentioned every day. Isn't that right?'

'Every day is an exaggeration.'

'Not much of one. She drip-dripped the poison of her own bitterness for years. You know she did. She couldn't get over the fact that he left her in the end, even though she'd put up with his roving eye most of their marriage.'

Melody lifted her soft chin and glared at him anew. 'And why should she have forgiven him? He was a hateful man. I'd have taken him to the vets for a certain operation if he'd been my husband,' she declared stoutly.

A flicker of a smile touched Zeke's mouth. 'I'll bear that in mind,' he said gravely. 'But the truth is her jaundiced view did some damage and made you very insecure in certain areas. Admit it. It's the truth, Dee, and you know it. Face it.'

'I'll do no such thing.' How dared he criticise her grandmother like this? 'And my father and grandfather's actions have absolutely nothing to do with this situation.'

'It isn't a situation, Dee,' Zeke said grimly. 'It's our marriage and, regardless of what you say, their unfaithfulness has a huge bearing on how you see it and me. Did you ever expect us to make old bones together? Did you? Deep, deep inside, in your subconscious? Because I don't think you did. I never have. But that didn't matter because I intended to prove you wrong and I wasn't going anywhere. I'm still not.'

He was confusing her, muddling everything up, and it wasn't fair. She had prepared herself for the inevitable over the past torturous weeks, steeling her heart against any hope, and she couldn't go back to the terrible time just after the accident when she hadn't known what to do. That had been worse than after she'd realised leaving Zeke was the only way she could retain her dignity and who she was in the future. She couldn't watch him slowly fall out of love with her as their life together went wrong. Their work and colleagues, their friends—*everything* was tied up in a world in which she had no part now. The very thing that had joined them was now the gulf forcing them apart. The ultimate irony.

'I just know I can't do this any more, Zeke,' she said wearily. 'Us, our marriage. I can't.'

The entrance doors to the hotel opened as she finished speaking and a young Japanese couple came in with two small and clearly very excited children, gabbling away in their own tongue. The little girls were so cute in their matching red coats and hats that in spite of how she was feeling Melody had to smile as she caught their mother's eye.

'It's the snow,' the young woman called across in perfect English. 'They so wanted snow at Christmas, so Santa and the reindeers could land their sleigh here and feel at home.'

'That's very important,' Melody agreed, glancing at the little tots as she added, 'And don't forget to leave some carrots for those reindeers, will you? They get very tired delivering so many presents in one night.'

The children giggled; whether they understood her or not Melody wasn't sure, but as she turned back to Zeke he was watching her with unfathomable eyes.

'And what about the family we said we'd have one day?' he said quietly. 'Where do children fit into this future of yours?'

She looked down at her hands, letting the heavy wings of soft strawberry-blond hair hide her face from him. 'They—they don't,' she whispered, knowing if she didn't have babies with Zeke she wouldn't have them with anyone. Just the thought of another man touching her was unthinkable. She was Zeke's and she'd always be his—body and soul—even though she couldn't be with him.

'I see.' His voice was low and tight. 'So you've made

the decision on my behalf. How kind. And am I allowed to protest at losing the chance of fatherhood?'

'You don't have to lose it. You could have children with someone else.' She still didn't look at him.

'If it wasn't for the fact we're in a public place I'd tell you exactly what I think of that little gem,' he ground out with hot, fuming fury. 'Do you seriously imagine anyone else could take your place? Do you? Hasn't anything I've said in the past meant something? I fell in love with *you*. I don't want anyone *but* you. Not ever. Listen to what I'm saying, damn it.'

She had never seen him so angry when she made the mistake of glancing up. His face was that of a stranger—a dangerous, outraged stranger—as black as thunder, and his words were underlined with the same furious energy.

Her heart threatened to give way but somehow she kept her voice steady when she said, 'This is what I was trying to avoid by not seeing you. I don't want to fight with you, Zeke, but I mean what I say and you won't change my mind. If you want to forget about lunch and leave now that's fine.'

She watched him slowly rein in his anger, his self-control formidable. She had seen it before, this ability to master his emotions, and it was almost scary. After a few moments he was able to smile slowly, and you would have to know him very well indeed to recognise it wasn't a real smile. But she did know him well.

'I'm here and I'm staying,' he drawled lazily.

And Melody had the feeling he wasn't only talking about lunch.

CHAPTER FOUR

THEY sat in a quivering silence that vibrated with things said and unsaid, until a young, pert receptionist came across to inform them smilingly that their table in the restaurant was waiting for them.

Melody had steadfastly kept her eyes on the view outside the windows, where the snow continued to fall thickly from a heavy, laden sky, but she was vitally aware of Zeke's black, brooding gaze fixed on her profile. In spite of his relaxed, nonchalant pose—one leg crossed over the other knee and his arms draped along the back of the sofa—she knew Zeke was as tense as a coiled spring.

The restaurant was pleasant enough, but nothing like the grand, expensive eating places Zeke had always taken her to. Nonetheless, the Christmas decorations were tasteful and brought a festive charm to the room, and their table for two was pretty, with a tiny beaded Christmas tree taking centre stage on a white linen tablecloth encrusted with sparkling silver stars.

After the waiter had placed two embossed menus in their hands and left them to decide on their meal, the wine waiter appeared. Zeke smiled at her. 'As we're celebrating, I think a bottle of your finest champagne,' he said to the waiter, but with his eyes on Melody.

The waiter beamed. This was obviously his type of customer. And at Christmastime too, when everyone tended to tip well.

Melody let the man bustle off before she said quietly, 'Celebrating?' keeping her voice expressionless.

'Of course. You're out of hospital and life can start again.' His smile was challenging. 'Isn't that worthy of good champagne?'

She wasn't going to rise to his bait, she told herself silently. Raising her small chin a notch, she shrugged. 'I didn't think you approved of drinking and driving.'

'Quite right,' he said with aggravating aplomb. 'I don't.'

Fighting the urge to ask what he was going to do about the Ferrari, because she knew he wanted her to do just that, Melody gritted her teeth and concentrated on the menu. No doubt he'd get one of his minions to pick up the car and he'd get a taxi home. He wouldn't care about spoiling someone's plans for Christmas Eve.

And then she immediately felt ashamed of herself. Whatever else Zeke was, he wasn't high-handed with his staff. She was just being nasty, and it wasn't like her. But then she'd come to realise over the past months since the accident that she didn't know herself at all.

She had always thought she was quite a focused, well-balanced person on the whole—the type of woman who would take whatever life threw at her and get on with things. But the accident had knocked her for six—not just physically but mentally, and more importantly emotionally too. It had been one of those cataclysmic events—one of those disasters that she hadn't imagined in her worst nightmares—and she hadn't known how to handle the fall-out. She still didn't. It had brought to the surface a whole host of emotional blocks which had begun to dissolve to reveal the insecurities and pain inside, starting from as way back as her father walking out on her and her mother. He obviously hadn't wanted the responsibility, so had he abandoned her mother because of that? Had she been the cause of their break-up?

Melody suddenly became aware that the waiter was back and pouring sparkling champagne into two crystal flutes. Once he'd placed the bottle in an ice bucket he sailed off again, and Zeke raised his glass to her. 'To you,' he said very softly. 'My beautiful, vulnerable, exasperating, sweet, incomparable wife. The centre of my universe.'

She had raised her own glass. Now she put it down without taking a sip. 'Don't, Zeke.' Her voice was quiet and pained.

'Don't what? Say how much I adore you? But I do, Dee.'

'You—you don't have to say that.' Her legs were hurting, reminding her of how she looked beneath her leggings.

'Have to?' His tone was quizzical rather than annoyed. He shook his dark head. 'When have I ever done anything because I have to? Okay, that toast clearly isn't to your liking. How about—' he raised his glass again and paused until she did the same '—to us?' he suggested mildly.

'Zeke.' She frowned at him but he merely smiled back.

'The season then. A merry Christmas to one and all. Is that sufficiently impersonal? Surely you can drink to that?'

Melody tasted the champagne. It was delicious, Dom Pérignon at its best, smooth, seductive and sophisticated—very much like Zeke. She glanced at him.

'Very nice,' she said primly, trying not to notice how his mouth was curving.

'Isn't it?' he agreed softly. 'Are you hungry?'

Surprisingly, for the first time since the accident, she did have something of an appetite. She nodded. 'A bit.'

'Good. You need feeding up.' Ignoring her grimace at the criticism of her thinness, he went on, 'I'm going to pass on the Christmas fare and save the turkey dinner till tomorrow. How about you? The salmon *en croûte* looks good for a starter, and the lamb shanks with red-currant and rosemary to follow for me, I think. I'll think about dessert later.'

Melody would have chosen the same, but felt the need to assert her independence. 'I'll have the wild mushroom pâté and then the beef in black bean sauce.' She put the menu down and took another sip of champagne. The bubbles danced in her mouth as the wine fizzed and she reflected she would have to be careful. She hadn't drunk any alcohol in the past months whilst in hospital, and this excellent vintage was as dangerous as it was delicious. With Zeke in the mood he was in she needed all her wits about her. She had never been able to resist him in the past, with or without alcohol.

The waiter glided to their table and as Zeke talked to him Melody was able to really study Zeke's face for the first time that morning. He looked as attractive as ever, but tired, she thought, a little dart of concern piercing her heart. Had he been working too hard? Before their marriage she'd heard it wasn't unknown for him to work round the clock when some drama or other necessitated it, and even after they'd wed there had been the odd occasion when she hadn't seen him for twenty out of twenty-four hours. He found it impossible to delegate, that was the thing. Having carved out his small empire with blood, sweat and tears, he was fiercely proud and protective of it, and not always so sure of himself as he'd like people to believe. Particularly so with regard to her.

It had been that which had first captivated her when they had begun dating, she acknowledged. He'd been mad for her but touchingly unsure of how she felt about him, which had surprised her. He rarely talked about his early days, but when he did she'd come to realise he'd had massive issues about love and commitment in the past and trusting the female of the species.

The thought bothered her. She had been trying to push such truths to the back of her mind these past weeks.

But Zeke *would* find someone else easily enough, she told herself in the next breath. Her grandmother had always said that love meant something entirely different to men and women, and that men's love was altogether more earthy and transient. 'Even the best of them will look for a younger, fitter model in time, Melody. Just you remember that and protect yourself against the day it happens.'

For a moment it was as though her grandmother was right there with her and Melody blinked, mentally shaking herself. Zeke had said her grandmother's jaundiced view of life and love had affected her, and she hadn't liked it at the time, but could there be some truth in it? Had it affected her adversely?

The idea felt like a betrayal of the woman who had raised her and sacrificed much to give her the dancing lessons she'd craved, and Melody immediately repudiated it. Men *did* obsess on a woman's body and looks. The number of middle-aged women who were dumped during their husbands' 'mid-life crisis' was proof of that. Men simply weren't naturally monogamous.

She came out of her reverie to find she'd inadvertently finished her glass of champagne and that Zeke's gaze was tight on her face. Silently he refilled her glass. 'What were you thinking just now?' he asked quietly. 'It was about me, wasn't it?'

There was no way she was going to tell him, but she had to say something to satisfy that razor-sharp mind. She made herself glance across the restaurant, which was gradually filling up, her stance studiously offhand, before she said, 'Just that today hasn't gone the way I'd planned, I suppose.'

'Did you really think after three months or so of being incarcerated I'd let you do this on your own?'

'I am more than capable of taking care of myself,' she said tersely. 'I'm not a child.'

His voice carried more than a touch of self-deprecation when he drawled, 'Believe me, Dee, I've never seen you as a child. Exasperating, unfathomable on occasion, but never a child.'

She flushed at the sensual desire in the ebony eyes. She'd walked right into that one. Flustered, she sipped at her champagne, before realising what she was doing and putting the glass down so abruptly it almost toppled over.

'Relax.' He took her hand, as if he had the perfect right to touch her whenever he wanted to and her talk of separation and divorce had never happened. 'You're like a cat on a hot tin roof. This is me, remember? Your husband.'

He slid his thumb into her curved palm, softly stroking her silky skin before turning her hand over and raising it to his lips. A bolt of electricity shot up her arm and she gasped before she could stifle her reaction to his mouth on her sensitive flesh. Jerking her hand away, she glared at him. 'Don't do that,' she said, a mite too fiercely.

'Another don't.' His mouth curved wryly. 'But you like me touching you. Don't deny it. And I like touching you, Dee. Remember how it used to be?' His gaze drifted to her lips and she felt them tingle, the tips of her breasts hardening as a flood of sexual need raced through her. 'We'd make love anywhere, any time, remember? And that's what we did, Dee. We made *love*. We didn't just have sex, great though that was.'

She wanted to say *Don't* again, and stopped herself just in time, but his voice was evoking memories she could have done without—memories that persisted in surfacing in dreams at night that rent her in two when she awoke and he wasn't there.

'Like that time in Madeira when you were cooking us pancakes for breakfast and we found another use for the maple syrup,' he murmured throatily. 'I swear I've never tasted anything so good. We never did have the pancakes, did we...?'

They had ravished each other right there on the sun-warmed wood of the kitchen floor, and later, when they'd showered away the stickiness of the syrup together, washing each other with silky-soft suds, they had made love again, slowly and languorously, making it last. Heady days. Magical days.

Aware that she was in a public place, and couldn't give way to the anguish the terrible enchantment of his words had induced, Melody grappled for self-control. It didn't matter how good they had been together. That was then and this was now. The girl who had revelled in winding her smooth, honey-coloured limbs round his, who had delighted in the pleasure he got from her perfect body, was no more. Never again would she feel so uninhibited, so full of joy, so *his*. She didn't expect him to understand—she barely understood herself—but self-survival dictated she had to leave him before she withered and died trying to be the person he'd fallen in love with. She couldn't face the prospect of kindness and pity replacing the desire and passion he'd had for her.

'You want me, Dee. Every bit as much as I want you.' He refused to accept her transparent self-denial. 'You need to feel me inside you as much as I need to be there. I want to make love to you for hours again. Nothing hasty or rushed, because we have all the time in the world now you're with me once more. Every doubt you have, every concern, I can make it better. I can sweep them all away and make you believe we're okay.'

'No, you can't, and I'm not with you again—not in the way you mean,' Melody said feverishly, trying to fight the ache of sexual need his words had called forth.

'You're mine, you'll always be mine, and you know it.' He leant closer, not touching her yet enveloping her with his body warmth. 'Our home is waiting for you and it's killing me to live there alone. I can't be there without imagining you in my arms, making love in every room like we did the first week we moved in.' His ebony gaze watched the way the memories he'd called up were sinking in, and his voice was husky as he continued softly, 'This is the first day of the rest of our lives together—'

'Stop it.' Her tone was sharp enough to check anything further he might have said. 'Stop it or I'm leaving right now.'

He stared into her eyes, large and tragic against her

pale features, and then swore under his breath. Leaning back in his seat, he drained his glass of champagne.

The waiter brought their first course to the table in the next few moments, and it was another minute or two, after they had begun to eat, that he said, his voice conversational, 'I don't know whether I want to kiss you or strangle you right now.' His voice was low, but she knew he meant every word.

'You don't need to worry about it because I wouldn't let you do either.' She deliberately kept her voice light and her face expressionless. 'This is wonderful pâté, by the way.'

Zeke's eyes were hard black stones as he tried to assimilate the change in her. She could see she had thrown him, and because he was always perfectly in control he wouldn't like that. She didn't think a woman had ever said no to him before either; until he had met her he had always been the one to end his relationships, and they had invariably been conducted exactly the way he decreed. Having said that, most of his exes seemed to have a soft spot for him still.

'So you are determined to continue with this ridiculous farce?' he said mildly, after he had finished his salmon.

Melody looked at him squarely, blessing the strength that had come from somewhere and was keeping her trembling inside under wraps. 'You mean the separation? Of course.'

'Of course?' he drawled lazily, his mood having taken a lightning change of direction. 'I wouldn't have said there was any "of course" about it. But what am I? A mere man.'

Melody eyed him warily. No one could accuse Zeke James of being a mere anything.

He stared back at her, his uneven mouth lifted in the appealing curve she knew so well. Why did he have to be so—so *everything*? she asked herself with silent despair. Why couldn't she have fallen in love with a nice Mr Average—someone *she* found attractive but who didn't have the rest of the female race champing at the bit? Someone she could have felt was truly hers?

But she hadn't. Bottom line. And maybe it wouldn't have made any difference to how she was feeling if she had. Maybe she would still feel she had to go it alone even if her man had been a nondescript nine-to-fiver with as much sex appeal as the average gnat. But she didn't think so.

Zeke refilled their glasses as the waiter whisked their empty plates away. Christmas carols were playing softly in the background, and outside the restaurant windows the small courtyard the room overlooked had been transformed into a winter wonderland, the one tree it contained proudly displaying its new clothing of glittering white. The flakes of snow, as thick and luscious as in a child's painting, were still falling fast, and already an inch or so carpeted the ground.

Without really thinking about what she was saying, she turned to Zeke. 'The snow's settling fast. As soon as you've eaten you ought to think about leaving.'

The hour's drive to their big sprawling manor house on the outskirts of Reading would take double the time in this weather, and the Ferrari—beautiful though it undoubtedly was—wasn't ideal for Arctic conditions. He could easily get stranded in the middle of nowhere.

Zeke's smile was little more than a quizzical ruffle. 'Can't wait to get rid of me?' he murmured.

He was at his most sexy in this mocking mood, but Melody refused to be charmed. 'That and the fact you could well find yourself stuck in the middle of a snow-drift somewhere. The wind's getting up—or hadn't you noticed?'

'I'd noticed.'

Melody shrugged. 'Don't say I didn't warn you.'

'Considering you've done nothing *but* warn me about things since first thing this morning, I wouldn't dream of it.'

He was still smiling, but she hadn't imagined the edge to his voice and it did nothing to reassure her he had decided to accept defeat. She felt a wave of intense weariness sweep over her for a moment. She didn't want to have to fight him. She felt so emotionally bruised and battered she just craved peace of mind, and she wouldn't achieve that until she was far, far away from Zeke. Once she had got herself together and organised a few essentials she intended to disappear for a few months. She wouldn't take a penny of his fortune to support herself—she had worked for her living in bars and restaurants before, and she could do it again, and she'd already thought about setting herself up as a dance teacher in the future.

The waiter appeared again with their main course, but suddenly her appetite was gone and she had to force herself to eat. It didn't help that Zeke was watching her like a hawk with its prey, his eyes boring into her as though he was trying to dissect her brain. Which he probably was, she reflected darkly. He would be look-ing for a chink in her armour—it was the nature of the beast.

'You're struggling.' As Melody glanced at him, Zeke motioned with his fork at her own plate. 'Tired?'

She nodded. The effort of leaving the hospital and not least this confrontation with Zeke, which she had been hoping to avoid until she was stronger, had taken more out of her than she would have thought possible. The doctors had predicted that she would experience bouts of extreme exhaustion in the early days of her release, but she hadn't expected to feel so completely wiped out. All she wanted to do was to crawl into bed.

'Want to skip dessert for now?' he asked softly.

She didn't know quite what he meant by 'for now', but was too weary to take him up on it. She had eaten more at one sitting than at any time over the past weeks, and the champagne had done its bit to drug her too. Dessert was beyond her. She nodded again. She could lay her head down and sleep right now.

Zeke lifted his hands. The waiter appeared at his side and within moments they were leaving the restaurant. She had known she was going to find it difficult to stand up and walk—her muscles still weren't functioning as they once had, and she got stiff easily although her physiotherapist had assured her that was just a temporary thing—but in the event Zeke's firm hands at her elbows and the way he took charge smoothed the way. Nevertheless, she was painfully aware of her pronounced limp as they left, and wondered what he was thinking. He had always said she had the grace of a young gazelle—well, no more, Melody thought wretchedly.

Once in the foyer of the hotel, she stopped and faced him so he was forced to let go of her arm. He was wearing an expensive dark grey suit and a pale peach shirt and tie and he had never looked more attractive. The dark magnetism that was at the centre of his appeal was so strong she could taste it. Numbly, and with formal politeness, Melody said, 'Thank you for lunch. It was very nice. And although it may not have seemed like it

I appreciate your kindness in meeting me from hospital today—although it wasn't necessary. I hope you have a good journey back to Reading.'

Zeke's jaw was a tight line, but his voice was easy when he said, 'You need to rest. I'll get the key to the room.'

'I can do that—' She stopped. She was talking to herself. He was already striding to the reception desk.

Too tired to summon up the annoyance she felt his high-handedness deserved, she watched him exchange a few words with the pretty receptionist before pocketing the fob for the room. Then he was back at her side, taking her arm as he said, 'I've ordered tea and cake from Room Service for four o'clock. That'll give you two or three hours' sleep, okay?'

Not okay. *So* not okay. What was he *doing*, taking charge like this after everything she'd said? 'Zeke—' she began.

'Don't cause a scene, Dee. Not with all these nice people round about. You don't want to spoil someone's Christmas, do you?' The mockery was mild, but with a hidden barb in it.

Short of wrenching herself free, which she had no confidence she could accomplish, anyway, Melody found she had no option but to walk with him to the lift. She didn't want Zeke accompanying her to the room. The foyer had been a fairly neutral place to make their goodbyes, with plenty of people around; her room was an altogether different proposition.

As it turned out it wasn't a problem, because once the lift had deposited them at the requisite floor and Zeke had walked a few yards down the corridor and opened a door Melody found he had no intention of leaving straightaway.

He stood aside for her to precede him, but she stopped dead on the threshold of what was clearly a suite of rooms. 'This isn't my room. I didn't book this,' she gasped. 'I asked for a standard double.' And *that* had cost an arm and a leg.

'You've clearly been upgraded,' he said silkily, drawing her into the large, luxuriously furnished sitting room, complete with real Christmas tree dressed in festive red and gold decorations, before her wits could return.

When they did, she swung to face him accusingly. 'This is your doing.' She glanced round wildly, as though the manager of the hotel was going to pop up like a genie out of a bottle. 'I want my own room. I want the one I booked originally.'

'I understand from the receptionist that was snapped up minutes after I transferred to this when we arrived,' Zeke said with unforgivable satisfaction. 'Look on it as your Christmas good deed. Those folk probably wouldn't have been able to afford this penthouse, which was the only other available accommodation when I asked, so us having it has meant a happy Christmas for someone else. It *is* the season of goodwill.'

Melody said something very rude in response, which shocked them both. And then the full significance of his words hit her. 'What do you mean, "us"?' she bit out furiously. 'This is my room and I'm staying in it alone—and I'll pay for it.' Somehow.

'Payment in full has already been made,' Zeke replied, seemingly unmoved by her anger.

'Well, it can be darn well unmade.'

'And cause the hotel staff a lot of extra paperwork and hassle?' Zeke clicked his tongue aggravatingly. 'You seem a little short of the milk of human kindness, if you don't mind me saying so. Hasn't the spirit of the festive season touched you?'

She had never come so close to hitting someone before, which shocked her further because she had never considered herself a violent person. Gritting her teeth, she took an audible deep breath. 'I want you to leave, Zeke. Right now.'

She had expected him to argue, so it took the wind out of her sails when instead he said mildly, 'Once you're safely in bed. And don't worry that I'm going to leap on you and have my wicked way. I can see you're dead on your feet, sweetheart.'

It was the way he said the last word which drained her of all resistance. Horrified that she was going to burst into tears, she said tersely, 'I'm going to the bathroom,' and walked as purposefully as she could manage across the room.

The suite consisted of a further three rooms—one a small study, complete with every device needed to keep in touch round the world for a visiting businessman or woman, and two bedrooms, both with *en-suite* bathrooms and decorated in the same creams and hazy greys and golds as the sitting room.

Walking into the cream marble *en-suite* of the second bedroom, Melody shut the door and stood for a moment with her eyes tightly closed. It was a sheer effort of will to open them and walk over to the long mirror. She groaned softly as she peered at her reflection. Her summer tan had long since faded after the months in hospital, but she had been careful to keep up with her cleansing and moisturising routine in spite of everything. Today, though, her skin looked pasty and almost grey with the exhaustion that was racking her body, and her green eyes looked enormous in her thin face. Not a pretty sight; no wonder Zeke had wanted to cut the meal short—she looked like death warmed up.

She had seen her case on the luggage rack in the bedroom as she'd marched through, but rather than go into the bedroom she stripped down to her bra and panties before pulling on the big fluffy white bathrobe which was one of two hanging on the back of the bathroom door. It drowned her, but that was all to the good, she decided, pulling the belt tightly round her slim waist. It concealed everything she needed to conceal from those piercing ebony eyes and that was all that mattered.

He was waiting for her when she padded barefoot into the sitting room, and as she said brightly, 'All ready for bed, as you can see, so you can go now,' his gaze swept over her from head to foot. She found she was doubly glad of the voluminous robe as her traitorous body responded, the rosy peaks of her breasts hardening.

Gruffly, Zeke said, 'You look tinier than ever in that thing. Was the hospital food really that bad?'

She shook her head. 'It was me. I didn't have much of an appetite, I suppose. I'll soon put the weight on again now.'

'Tiny, but beautiful.' His voice was husky now, his face telling her what his words didn't. 'Enchantingly so, in fact.'

It was this she answered when she murmured, 'Please go, Zeke. I can't…' She swallowed hard. 'Please leave.'

'I know, I know.' He took her hands in his, pulling her against the broad wall of his chest and nuzzling the top of her head with his chin. 'You need to rest. You've done too much for your first day out.'

In spite of herself Melody smiled. 'You make it sound as thought I've just been released from prison,' she whispered, her voice muffled against his shirt. Which was how she felt, actually. And then she pulled away, the smell and feel of him too wonderfully familiar. She wanted to wrap her arms round his neck, to feel his lips on hers, to beg him to forget everything she'd said and hold her tight. 'Please go,' she said again, her voice trembling.

He lifted his hand and stroked a strand of silky hair from her cheek. She thought he was going to kiss her, and when he merely brushed her brow with his lips knew a moment's agonising disappointment.

'Sweet dreams,' he said very softly. 'Don't forget the tea and cake around four.'

She nodded, not really believing he would go like this, that he would leave her. She watched him cross the room and open the door into the corridor outside, all the time expecting that any moment he would swing round and come back to her. But he didn't.

The door closed. She was alone. Which was exactly what she had demanded.

CHAPTER FIVE

MELODY stood staring across the room for some moments, fighting the urge to run after Zeke and say...

Say what? she asked herself wearily. That she had changed her mind? But she hadn't. Not about leaving him. All her reasons held good for that, and had perhaps deepened in the past hours since she had seen him again. She loved him too much, and his power over her had always scared her a little deep inside the private place in her mind where uncomfortable truths were buried. She had to get far away from him. That was the only way.

She swayed a little, so tired she could barely remain upright, and then made her way into the bedroom where her case had been left earlier. Shrugging off the robe, she climbed into bed, wanting to think about her and Zeke, to reaffirm to herself the rationale that vindicated her decision, but so exhausted her brain simply wouldn't compute. She couldn't think. Not now.

The swirling snow outside the bedroom window had bathed the room in soft evening shadow, despite it being only a little past one o'clock, and the bed was supremely comfortable after the hard institutional one she had endured for the past three months. Within seconds her breathing was even and deep and she slept a dreamless sleep.

She was completely unaware of the big broad figure that entered the room a few minutes later, standing just inside the doorway until he had satisfied himself her sleep was genuine, at which point he walked softly over to the bed. Zeke stared down at his sleeping wife for several long minutes, his gaze caressing the fragility of her fine features as she slept, and the breakable quality of the shape under the coverlet.

When he noiselessly closed the drapes against the worsening storm outside the cosy cocoon of the hotel his cheeks were damp.

Melody wasn't sure exactly what had dragged her out of the depths of a slumber so heavy her limbs were weighed down with it. She lay in a deep, warm vacuum, a charcoal twilight bathing the room in indistinct shapes as she forced her eyes open. She felt blissfully, wonderfully relaxed.

For a moment she had no idea where she was, and then the past few hours came rushing back at the same time as voices somewhere beyond the bedroom registered. Male voices.

She couldn't remember closing the curtains. She stared towards the window, her brain still fuzzy, but then as familiar deep tones registered she sat up in bed, shaking her hair out of her eyes. *That was Zeke's voice.* She glanced at her wristwatch but it was too dark to make out the time.

Her heart thudding fit to burst, she threw back the coverlet and reached for her robe on the chair at the side of the bed, pulling it on with feverish haste. After switching on the bedside lamp she again checked her watch. Four o'clock. Tea and cake. Room Service. But that still didn't explain what Zeke was doing here—unless she had imagined it, of course.

Zeke was very real when she opened the door to the sitting room. Too real. Melody's senses went into hyperdrive as she registered the very male body clad only in black silk pyjama bottoms. Not that Zeke had ever worn pyjamas to her knowledge.

It was clear he'd just had a shower before answering the door. His thickly muscled torso gleamed like oiled silk where he hadn't dried himself before pulling on the pyjama bottoms, and the black hair on his chest glistened with drops of water. He was magnificent. Melody had forgotten just how magnificent, but now she was reminded—in full, glorious Technicolor.

She swallowed hard, telling herself to say something. *Anything.* But her thought process was shattered.

'Hi.' His smile was ridiculously normal in the circumstances. 'Did the knock at the door wake you? It's our tea and cake.'

She tried, she *really* tried to rise to the occasion, as one of the sophisticated beauties he'd dated before he'd met her would have done, but she knew she'd failed miserably when her voice held the shrillness of a police car siren. *'What are you doing here?'* she yelled. 'You're supposed to have left.'

His expression changed to one of wounded innocence, which was all the more unbelievable in view of his attire—or lack of it. Before he could voice the reasonable and utterly false explanation she just *knew* was hovering on his lips, she continued, 'And why is the tea and cake for two, considering you ordered it hours ago?'

'Ah...' He smiled, a smile of singularly sweet ingenuousness. 'I can explain.'

'Please do,' she said with biting sarcasm.

'I never intended for you to be alone on Christmas Eve, so I thought I'd stick around for a while, that's all.'

He raked back his hair, which had fallen quiff-like across his brow, and she was reminded how much it suited him that bit longer than he normally wore it before she hastily pushed the thought aside. 'I didn't invite you to stay,' she glinted angrily. 'And why are you dressed—' perhaps *un*dressed would have been a more appropriate description '—like this?'

He glanced down at the pyjama bottoms, as though he was surprised at the obviousness of the question, and then met her furious gaze with a serenity that sent Melody's stress level up a few more notches. 'I was having a shower when Room Service came with the tea and cake,' he said patiently.

Melody hung on to *her* patience by a thread. 'Why were you taking a shower in my hotel room?' she said tersely. 'And how come your pyjamas are here?'

'I was taking a shower in *my* room—you notice this suite has two bedrooms?' His tone was such he could have been talking to a total dimwit. 'And I went out and bought the pyjamas and a couple of other bits while you were asleep. I assumed you'd prefer me to wear something to answer the door in the sort of situation that just occurred,' he added, his tone so reasonable she wanted to hit him.

Glaring at him, she wondered how she had lost control of things. It had all been so straightforward earlier that morning. Leave the hospital. Book into the hotel. Go to bed and hibernate Christmas away. And now look at what a ridiculous position she was in—her estranged husband sharing a hotel suite with her and standing practically naked a few feet away.

And looking hot. The little voice in the back of her mind was ruthlessly honest. In fact he was fairly smoking. Zeke had always been very much at ease with his body, and it enhanced his flagrant masculinity tenfold. Wretched man.

Pulling herself together, Melody hardened her heart as well as her expression. 'You said you were leaving earlier,' she said stonily. 'And I expected you to do just that.'

He gave her a crooked smile as he sat down on one of the sofas in front of the glass coffee table where their tea and cake were waiting. 'No,' he corrected softly. 'I never did. I know that because wild horses couldn't have dragged me away. I would have preferred us to go home and discuss what needs to be discussed there, but that clearly wasn't going to happen. So—' he shrugged broad muscled shoulders and Melody's mouth went dry '—I adapted to the circumstances as I saw fit.'

'Hence changing the room to a suite?' she said stiffly.

'Quite. We may as well be comfortable for as long as this charade continues.' He grinned happily. 'These cakes look fantastic. I've always been a sucker for chocolate cupcakes and fondant fancies—and that's a lemon drizzle cake, if I'm not mistaken. We missed dessert, so come and tuck in.' He was pouring two cups of tea as he spoke.

Melody hesitated for a moment. She wasn't going to give in, and there was no way Zeke was sharing this suite tonight, but the assortment of cakes *did* look tempting, and surprisingly—for the second time that day—she found she was actually quite hungry. She would have preferred Zeke to be fully dressed, but as he seemed more interested in the food than in her...

She sat down on the opposite sofa, accepting the cup

of tea he handed her with a nod of thanks and selecting one of the little pink-and-white Genoese sponge fondant fancies hand-decorated with sugar daisies. It melted in her mouth, and when Zeke offered her the cakestand again she took a piece of lemon drizzle cake, filled with rich buttercream and lemon curd, refusing to acknowledge how cosy this was.

Outside the snow was coming down thicker than ever, and as she glanced at the window Melody's stomach did a pancake flip. It was too late to send Zeke away. He'd never make it to Reading now, she acknowledged silently. Okay, so maybe he *would* have to stay after all, but strictly on her terms—and that included his and hers bedrooms first and foremost.

She glanced at him from under her eyelashes. He was sitting eating with every appearance of relaxed enjoyment, and after she had declined more cake had made short work of what was left on the cake stand. The man was impossible—utterly impossible.

He glanced up and caught her looking at him, and as always when he smiled at her in a certain way her blood fizzed. 'Remember when you made that clementine, saffron and polenta cake in Madeira?' he murmured softly. 'I haven't tasted anything so good as that before or since. You promised you'd make it again back in England, but you never did.'

The memory of that day at the villa in Madeira swept over her. It had been their last holiday before her accident and they'd had a magical time: horse-riding along the beach, scuba-diving, sunbathing in the shade of the trees around their private pool and spending each soft, scented night wrapped in each other's arms. They had bought the small juicy clementines at the little local market close to the villa, and she had followed a rec-

ipe which Aida—Zeke's daily from the village—had
written down for her. Melody was the first to admit
she wasn't much of a cook—Zeke was actually much
better than her, and had a natural flair with food that
made most dishes he served up truly sensational—but
the cake had turned out surprisingly well and Zeke had
been lavish with his praise.

They had eaten the moist, wonderfully tangy cake
after dinner with their coffee, sitting on the villa's balcony in the richly perfumed air as a glorious sunset had
filled the sky with rivulets of scarlet, gold and deep
violet, and afterwards, content and sated, had made
love for hours in their big, billowy bed. He'd told her
she was exquisite, a goddess…

Enough. The warning was loud in her head. That
was then and this was now, and the girl who had lived
in a bikini practically the whole holiday was gone. She
had never considered herself particularly beautiful, but
had always had confidence in her firm, graceful dancer's body, able to hold her own in that regard with the
jet-set who congregated around Zeke like moths to a
flame. What would they say now?

People. Melody's green eyes darkened. Always
people. When she thought about it now, she had never
felt she had Zeke completely. There had always been
people in the background making claims on him. Even
in Madeira there were friends who came by for dinner
or barbecues—beautiful people, rich, funny, intelligent,
fascinating. She had told herself she had to expect that;
he was nearly forty years old, for goodness' sake, and
he had built a life for himself that had to continue when
she had come along. It would have been totally unreasonable to expect anything else. And she hadn't minded

then—not much, anyway. Only sometimes she'd felt on the outside looking in.

'What's the matter?' He was staring at her. 'What is it?'

She came back from the past to find she must have been looking at him without seeing him. 'Nothing,' she said quickly. 'My mind was wandering, that's all.'

'Wherever it had wandered it didn't seem to be a good place from the look on your face.' His gaze narrowed. 'What makes me think it was something to do with us?' he added softly, leaning back in the sofa as he surveyed her through glittering black eyes. 'It was, wasn't it? What was it?'

Her senses registered the way his powerful muscles moved as sleekly as an animal's, and she was reminded again how magnificent his body was. The first time she had seen him naked she had been in awe of his male beauty. She still was.

'Melody?' he pressed silkily, in a way she knew meant he wasn't going to let the matter drop. 'Tell me.'

Suddenly she threw caution to the wind. 'I was thinking about how in the whole of our marriage, apart from on our honeymoon, we were constantly surrounded by people wanting a piece of you,' she said flatly. 'Weekdays, weekends—it was always the same. Looking back, I've sometimes thought I was just one of many hangers-on in your world.'

To say she had shocked him was an understatement. She watched as his fiercely intelligent mind considered what she'd said. 'You were never, ever *just* anything. As my wife you were up there with me one hundred per cent. Or at least I thought you were.' He had sat up straight as he'd spoken, every line of his body tense now. 'Obviously I was mistaken.'

She wasn't going to let him lay it all on her. 'You never asked me what I wanted, Zeke. Not really. And I admit for my part I should have spoken up, but I was overwhelmed by it all.' *By my incredible fortune in marrying you. By the impossible fact that you loved me.* 'And I'm not saying I didn't enjoy it, because I did, but I never really felt—'

'What? What didn't you feel?'

'That I fitted in, I guess.' She shook her head, biting her lip. 'Maybe you were right when you said I never thought we'd last. I was never conscious of thinking that, but once you said it I realised there was an element of truth there. And it wasn't just because of my grandmother and her attitude to men. Not wholly. It was because I sort of slotted into your life without you having to make any changes, with me hardly making a dent in your way of going on. And if I disappeared out of it again the same would apply. Nothing would really alter. I'd barely make a ripple as I left.'

Zeke was staring at her as though he'd never seen her before. 'You *can't* believe that,' he said eventually, clearly stricken. 'How many times did I tell you I loved you? That I had never loved anyone else? Did you think I was lying?'

Melody paused before answering. She was aware she had opened a can of worms, but there was no going back now. 'No, I know you loved me,' she said slowly. 'But why wouldn't you when I was doing everything you wanted? Being what you wanted? And it wasn't all your fault. I'm not saying that. I loved seeing how the other half lived and being part of that world. It was exhilarating and crazy and a million things besides. But—' Another silence while she searched for words to explain the unexplainable. 'But there's another world too—a real world. A world devoid of rose-coloured glasses.'

'Meaning what, exactly?' His voice was grim, his body tense.

She shrugged. 'I suppose I mean that outside the Zeke James bubble people struggle to pay their bills each month, they work nine to five just to make ends meet, they strive all their lives and never really make it. They can't just pick up the phone and have half a dozen people ready to jump through hoops and pave the way for whatever they want. They've never experienced walking into a store and being able to buy whatever they like without looking at the price tag. They have bad days, they get sick, they—they have accidents.'

She stopped abruptly. She wasn't putting this very well. What she wanted to say had nothing to do with wealth and fortune. Not really. It was about Zeke belonging to her and she to him. 'I can't explain it very well,' she added lamely.

'Are you blaming me for succeeding in life?' Zeke asked, his voice as even as a sheet of glass. 'Because you'll wait one hell of a long time for me to apologise for that. I pulled myself out of the gutter inch by inch, and I saw enough to know I'd rather slit my own throat than go back to it. Try living in a succession of rooms with the one person who's supposed to love and look after you but who forgets you're alive most of the time. Sleeping in filthy beds, eating half-mouldy food because if you don't you'll starve and no one will give a damn. Having no idea what a bath is but knowing other people out there don't smell like you and your mother and her pals do. And when you're finally dumped into care, longing to go back to that life, bad as it was, because it's all you've ever known and you're scared out of your wits.'

As if he couldn't bear looking at her he stood up, turning away and taking a deep breath. For a moment his back was ramrod-straight and the muscles in his shoulders hard and tense. Every line in his body proclaimed how much she'd hurt him.

Horrified at the wounds she'd uncovered, Melody murmured, 'Zeke, I'm sorry. I didn't mean... I'm sorry.'

He swung to face her and she saw the iron control was back. 'It doesn't matter.' His face was relaxed, calm, but she knew he wasn't feeling like that inside. 'It was a long time ago. But don't tell me I haven't experienced life, Dee. I wasn't brought up in what you call the Zeke James bubble. Blood, sweat and tears got me to where I am today—that and Lady Luck. But I'll tell you one thing.' He moved over to where she was now standing, his dark eyes fixed on hers. 'I could give it all up tomorrow and walk away without a backward glance or an ounce of regret. You talk about my world, but let me make one thing perfectly clear. It doesn't own me. I own it. There's a difference. One hell of a difference.'

Melody stared into the rugged face. She wanted to believe him but she didn't know if she did. And, anyway, did it really make any difference one way or the other? It was all relative.

This close, she was aware of the fresh soapy smell emanating from his body, of his still-damp hair falling into the quiff which was somewhat boyish and incongruous against the hard tough features. It strengthened his overwhelming maleness in a way that caused her heart to pound as the intimacy of the moment deepened. She felt the pull of his attraction drawing her.

He reached out and sifted a strand of her hair through

his fingers, letting it fall back into the shining curtain on her shoulders as his eyes caressed her face. 'You look good enough to eat,' he said huskily. 'Far more delicious than fondant fancies and infinitely more satisfying.'

Melody knew what was going to happen, and she also knew he was giving her time to move away, to break the spell which had fallen. The sitting room was lit only by a couple of lamps Zeke had switched on, and the soft mellow glow was enhanced by the swirling snow outside the window and the twinkling white lights on the little Christmas tree. It was cosy and snug, safe and warm, and the power of his sensuality wrapped round her as she gave herself up to the magic of his kiss.

His bare arms folded round her waist, tugging her into the cradle of his hips as he purposefully deepened the onslaught on her senses. She felt her breasts respond as the towelling robe pressed against the wall of his chest, their tips hardening and swelling as the blood heated in her veins.

His tongue probed the warmth of her inner mouth and the effect on her was electric. A little moan escaped her throat, vibrating against his mouth and causing Zeke to groan in return as her arms wound round his neck, her fingers sliding into the black thickness of his hair.

Now his mouth was hungry, demanding and wonderfully, achingly familiar as every nerve in her body sensitised. His grip tightened around her waist, his hips grinding against hers as he moved her against him. She arched in unconscious abandonment, unaware the folds of the robe had opened as her belt had loosened. And then she felt his warm hands on the bare flesh beneath the thin wispy bra she was wearing and she froze.

'No.' Her voice was high with panic as she jerked

away, pulling the robe back in place and jerking the belt tight.

Zeke was breathing like a long-distance runner and he had to take a rasping breath before he could speak. 'It's all right.' He wouldn't let her escape him completely, drawing her back into his embrace with steel-like arms which allowed no protest. 'We can take this as slow as you want.'

'I don't want it at all.' Melody's mouth was dry and she licked her lips and swallowed painfully. 'We can't—'

'We can.' He kissed her again—a mere brushing of her trembling mouth. 'We're man and wife, Dee, and you've just proved you want me every bit as much as I want you.' It wasn't arrogant or triumphant, just a simple statement of fact. 'We are one and you can't fight that.'

She shook her head dazedly, a hundred and one conflicting emotions tearing her apart. If they made love, if he saw her naked, he couldn't fail to be repulsed. And she couldn't bear that. She wanted him to remember her as she had been—to picture her in his mind as smooth-skinned, nubile, inviting. She was doing this for him as much as her. She *was*. He had married her when she was perfect. Why should he have to learn to adapt to anything less? She was finding it hard, but what would it do to a man like Zeke? No, this was the only way. It had to end now. Swiftly, cleanly, unhesitatingly—like the surgeon's scalpel. She had to remain strong. She couldn't weaken.

'No, Zeke,' she whispered. 'We're not man and wife any more. Not here, in my head.'

'I don't believe that.' He still continued to hold her, but now the circle of his arms was relaxed. 'Not for a minute, a second. So don't waste your breath trying to convince me when all you're really doing is lying to yourself, okay? Now, go and pamper yourself—have a long soak in the tub and cream and titivate and whatever else women do when they're getting ready for a night on the town. I'm wining and dining you tonight, and I've got tickets for the theatre.'

Melody stared at him aghast. 'I'm not going out.'

'Of course you are. We're not going to let a bit of snow beat us. This is London, not the arctic.'

'I don't mean that.' And he knew it. 'I'm staying here.'

'Why?' The ebony eyes challenged her. 'Why is that?'

Melody fell back on one of the oldest excuses in the book—the one that came just after *I've got a headache*. 'I've got nothing to wear,' she said. It was true. Her suitcase contained the leggings and T-shirts and other comfy clothes she had worn in hospital once she was allowed her own things, but absolutely nothing suitable for the sort of evening Zeke had described. All her evening things were back at their house.

He grinned. 'No problem.' Releasing her, he walked over to the Christmas tree and she saw that at some point during the afternoon a host of beautifully wrapped parcels had appeared beneath it. 'You can have a couple of your Christmas presents early,' he said cheerfully, extracting two parcels from the pile. 'I bought a size below your normal measurements, so hopefully they'll fit. Try them on and see.'

Utterly taken aback, Melody stuttered, 'When—? How—?'

Zeke paused as an array of emotions—wariness, delight, embarrassment—flitted across his features. 'I did a little shopping when you were asleep,' he admitted. 'I'd left your Christmas presents at home. I thought—' He shook his head. 'Well, you know what I thought. I didn't expect we'd be spending Christmas in a hotel in the city.'

'Zeke, I can't accept these.' It seemed absolutely brazen to take anything from him in the circumstances. 'You must see that.'

'Why not?' he said easily and without heat.

Melody wasn't fooled. She'd seen the flash of granite in his eyes.

'I just can't,' she murmured helplessly. 'I haven't got anything for you, for a start. It—it wouldn't be right.'

He slung the parcels on a sofa and reached for her again, refusing to let her go when she tried to pull away. One hand took hold of her face gently, lifting her chin so his midnight-dark eyes stared straight into hers. 'You being able to walk out of that place today is all the present I'll ever want. In those first few days I didn't think you were going to make it. I was terrified and I couldn't do anything. Something like that has a way of sorting out the priorities of life, believe me. So, you're my Christmas gift this year.'

'Zeke—' She was struggling not to cry. 'I can't—'

'I know, I know.' He pressed a quick kiss on her mouth. 'You don't want to hear it, but tough—it's the truth. Now, take your presents and go and make yourself even more beautiful, if that's possible. Because we *are* going out tonight, Dee. Even if I have to dress you myself.' He smiled, but Melody knew he wasn't joking. 'Which, incidentally, is the option I prefer.'

Knowing she ought to be stronger, but still melting from the beautiful things he'd said, she continued to stand looking at him for a moment more. Maybe going out was the best idea after all. Certainly a night in together would be dangerously cosy with Zeke in this impossibly seductive mood.

As if to confirm her thoughts Zeke kissed her again, as though he couldn't help himself—a kiss of slow sensuality. She had wedged her arms between them, flattening her palms on his powerful chest in an effort to push away from the hot desire which had immediately gripped her. It had always been the same; he only had to touch her and she was lost. His mouth moved to one shell-like ear, nibbling it before progressing to her throat and finding her pounding pulse. His rapid-fire heartbeat under her palms revealed Zeke's arousal as blatantly as the silk pyjama bottoms, and for a split second the old thrill and delight that she could inspire such desire in him was there, before a flood of cold reality doused the feeling as effectively as a bucket of icy water.

He didn't know what she looked like under the robe. He hadn't seen the scars and puckered skin.

Melody jerked away so violently she took him by surprise. 'Please don't,' she said brokenly. 'Please, Zeke.' She gathered up the parcels he'd thrown on the sofa and moved to the door, turning in the doorway to say, 'What time do I need to be ready?' as she nerved herself to look at him.

He hadn't moved, and her breath caught in her throat at the sheer male beauty of his magnificent body. The velvet eyes swept over her and there was no annoyance in his face. His voice was deep and warm and very sensual when he said, 'I've ordered cocktails here in the room for seven before we go.'

She nodded stiffly, holding the tears at bay through sheer willpower as it came to her that she had never loved him so much as she did right at this moment.

He was everything she had ever wanted—would ever want—and she was going to let him go. She knew it. She just had to make him believe it before she went insane trying.

CHAPTER SIX

Once in her own bedroom, Melody shut the door and plumped down on the bed, the parcels in her lap. She stared down at them through the mist of tears clouding her vision. Rubbing her hand across her eyes, she sniffed. *No crying. Not now. Not until this is over.* She couldn't give in. She had to be strong.

The short pep talk helped. She had always known life after the accident, particularly the first few days and weeks, was going to be hard. For all sorts of reasons.

She nodded to the thought. No just because of learning to cope with the world outside the hospital cocoon. She realised this confrontation with Zeke had always been on the cards from the moment she'd made up her mind their relationship was over. If she could have done she would have simply disappeared out of his life; she didn't want to argue or discuss or rationalise, but she had always accepted she would have to.

The fingers of her right hand moved slowly over the rings on her left, but she refused to brood on the day when she had chosen her engagement and wedding rings. Instead she opened the presents Zeke had given her. The silver shot-silk trousers were exquisite and the cream-and-silver tunic top more so; she didn't dare contemplate what they must have cost, but the designer label shouted exclusivity.

She wished he hadn't done this. Shutting her eyes for a moment, she let her shoulders slump—but it didn't help the tension gripping her nerves. She felt as though any minute now she was going to shatter into a thousand pieces, all the benefit of the afternoon sleep she'd enjoyed ruined.

Bath, she told herself, slightly hysterically. She'd wash the last of the hospital out of her hair and skin. Strange how the faintly antiseptic smell permeated everything, not matter how many creams and perfumes you applied. But she was free of all that now—free of the endless routine and doctor's visits and lack of privacy. So why did her heart feel even heavier, like a ton of bricks suspended in her chest? She had to pull herself together. She couldn't let Zeke affect her like this. If she wasn't strong now it would make things even harder in the future. This was just one night. She could get through that.

Leaving the clothes on the bed, she walked into the *en-suite* and began to run a bath, using a liberal amount of hotel bath oil until the water was a mass of perfumed bubbles. Slipping off the robe, she divested herself of her bra and panties before sliding into the foam until only her head was visible. It was only then, when her limbs and body were concealed, that she began to relax in the delicious silky warmth.

After the months in hospital there was an element of bliss in being able to luxuriate in the scented bubbles without fear of one of the nurses knocking on the door and asking her if she was all right. Not that she hadn't appreciated their kindness and concern—she had—but she had felt stifled at times.

How long she lay there she wasn't sure, but after a while the thought that time was getting on caused a little panic, and she quickly washed her hair and climbed out of the bath. In the old days she and Zeke had often unwound after work by taking a bath together, the room lit by candlelight and a bottle of their favourite wine in hand. It had been a great start to the evening—especially as their intimate sojourns in the massive sunken bath in their *en-suite* had invariably led to something else. They'd often eaten late by candlelight in their bathrobes.

But that was then and this was now, and trips down memory lane were both dangerous and weakening.

Melody's mouth twisted with pain and she pulled on her robe, jerking the belt tightly round her waist. There was no going back and it would be emotional suicide to try. She could no longer live up to Zeke's expectations—his and all the rest of the showbiz crowd they mixed with. And she didn't want to destroy herself attempting to do so. Oh, she didn't doubt most people would be very polite and sympathetic to her face, and some of them would even be genuine. But she had come up through the ranks and she knew how it was, how bitchy and calculating ambitious beauties like Katie could be. She couldn't live with the waiting. Waiting for one woman, more special or more clever at getting what she wanted than the rest, to draw Zeke in.

She wound her hair into a towel and then looked at her reflection in the mirror. Maybe that woman would never appear—perhaps Zeke would be strong against all the come-ons and remain faithful—but that was almost beside the point. It was *her* who would damage what they had if she stayed with him. She knew that now. Jealousy and suspicion were terrible things, and she couldn't expect Zeke to live with them and her, because that was how it would be. She had found out a lot about herself in the past weeks, and even more since she had seen him again today, and she wasn't proud of it. But it *was* reality.

Maybe if she didn't love him so much, or had had a different upbringing, or a thicker skin… She shook her head and turned from the bereft face in the mirror. Too many maybes. The accident had thrown up a whole host of gremlins buried deep in her psyche, and the only thing in the world she was sure about right now was that she had to step out of her life and begin again somewhere far away. And she could do that. She *would* do it. And then perhaps she could sort out her head. Given time. Find the courage to fight the deadening apathy that dominated her outlook on the future when she looked down long years without Zeke. In fact she'd have to. End of story.

She dressed quickly, relaxing infinitesimally once she was covered up. She didn't think Zeke would barge into the bedroom unannounced, in view of all that had been said, but…

She dried her hair into a sleek shining curtain either side of her face before applying her make-up. She kept it simple—just a touch of eyeshadow and mascara to enhance her green eyes and a warm plum-coloured lipstick for her lips. Nevertheless, the effect was almost startling after not wearing make-up for so long. Titivating had been the last thing on her mind in hospital, but now she looked at herself in the bedroom mirror and decided she would do the same every day.

Part of her rehabilitation, she thought with grim humour, remembering the words of the consultant when she had last seen him. He had been so kind, Mr Price.

Grey-haired and fatherly, but a man who called a spade a spade, albeit with compassion and gentleness. 'I've mended your body, Melody, but it's up to you to do the same with your spirit. I know this has knocked you for six, but there's the rest of your life to live now—which is more than some of my patients can look forward to. I don't understand everything you're feeling, but when you are ready I'd like you to see a colleague of mine who can talk things through with you as many times as you need.'

She'd looked down at the name and telephone number he had given her. Dr Greg Richardson. Swallowing hard, she had whispered, 'Is he a psychiatrist?' already knowing the answer. They all thought she was losing it, that she'd cracked.

Mr Price's voice had been soft when he'd answered. 'He is someone who works with people who need a different kind of healing to the one I can give. Look at it like that. He's a good man. More than that, he's a friend of mine and I know you would benefit from seeing him. Don't dismiss it out of hand, Melody. And...' The good doctor had paused, waiting until she had met his steady gaze before he'd continued, 'Don't make any life-changing decisions in the next little while. Give yourself time. It might be a cliché, but time is a great healer.'

'You're talking about Zeke,' she'd said woodenly.

This time the pause had been longer. 'Partly, yes.'

Mr Price had meant well. Turning away from the mirror, Melody took a deep breath. And she knew he hadn't agreed with her decision to end her marriage. Emotion flooded in, overwhelming her. But he didn't understand. How could he? He was a doctor first and foremost. He didn't have a clue about the entertainment industry other than what he experienced when he watched TV or went to the cinema or theatre. Showbiz was another world, a world within the everyday world, and since she had entered it after leaving dance school she had relished every second. It had been hard, exacting, unforgiving, sometimes unfair and often capricious, but it had enabled her to do what she loved most—dance. Or what she had loved most until she had met Zeke. From that point he'd become the centre of her world.

She had had it all. She bit her bottom lip with small white teeth, her eyes cloudy. And the gods didn't like mere mortals who tasted paradise on earth. How many times had she thought it was all too good to last? Well, she had been right. It hadn't lasted.

Melody stared blindly across the room, straightening her shoulders as she took several deep calming breaths. And now she had to adapt to the cards she'd been dealt. It was a simple as that. Everything was changed, but there were millions of other people much worse off than she was. She could not, she *would* not give in to the numb, grey, terrifying depression that kept trying to draw her into a mindless vacuum. There was life after dancing. There was life after Zeke.

'Melody?'

The knock at her bedroom door made her jump out of her skin as she came out of the maelstrom of her thoughts. Her hand at her chest, she steadied herself. Then she walked to the door and opened it, a cool smile stitched in place. 'I'm ready.'

He looked fabulous. Dinner suit, hair slicked back, magnetism increased tenfold. 'Hi,' he said softly. 'Cocktails in the sitting room? They're all ready.'

'Lovely.' Her voice was a little breathless but she

hoped he wouldn't notice. She needed to project cool-ness, if anything.

'You look…' He smiled and the warmth in his eyes increased her heartbeat to a gallop. 'Good enough to eat,' he finished huskily. 'But then you always do.'

'Thank you.' Even to her own ears her voice sounded ridiculously prim. 'The clothes are very nice.'

'But I forgot to give you this when I gave you the other things earlier.' He handed her a package, beauti-fully wrapped like the previous ones. He seemed totally at ease and not at all bothered by her lack of enthusiasm at the gift.

'What is it?' Melody asked flatly, refusing to ac-knowledge to herself how wildly attractive he was.

He took her arm, leading her through into the sitting room before he said quietly, 'Open it and see.'

'I—I don't want it. I mean, you've given me enough. I can't accept anything else. Not—not when I haven't got you—'

'Open it.' He interrupted her stumbling words coolly, and when she still made no attempt to obey him he ca-sually pushed her down on one of the sofas and sat be-side her, undoing the ribbons on the large box. 'It won't bite,' he added.

As he lifted the lid, Melody gazed down at the silver boots the box contained. The soft leather was worked with tiny crystals in a curling design that wound from toe to heel in a thin line on the outer side of each boot, and she would have known immediately—even if she hadn't seen the name on the box—that they'd cost an arm and a leg. She didn't remove the boots from their bed of tissue paper, raising her eyes to Zeke before she spoke. 'I can't accept these. I mean it, Zeke. I don't want anything else.'

He sat back a little, folding his arms over his chest as he surveyed her with an air of deceptive meekness. 'Why not?'

'I shouldn't have taken the clothes,' she said by way of answer, feeling churlish but knowing she had to make him see.

'But you did,' he pointed out gently, 'and these are part of that gift.' His eyes lowered to the black leather boots she was wearing, which were definitely more serviceable than anything else and couldn't compare to the exotic creations in the box.

Melody's mouth tightened as her chin rose. She knew what he was thinking, but he either took her out in her old boots or not at all. 'I'm sorry, Zeke. They're beautiful, but no.'

The mockery in the black eyes showed he was fully aware of what she was thinking. 'No problem,' he said lazily. 'If you change your mind before we leave they're here.'

'I won't.' She stood up abruptly. Sitting so close, she could smell the expensive sensual aftershave he favoured, and it was playing havoc with her thought process.

Zeke rose too, walking across to where a tray holding two glasses of her favourite cocktail—sapphire martini—was waiting. He handed her one of the frosted martini glasses full of the chilled gin and blue liqueur. 'No toasts tonight, but I hope you enjoy the evening,' he said softly. 'We're eating after the theatre, if that's okay? I thought it would give us time to work up an appetite after all that cake.'

Melody took a sip of the cocktail. The very blue, very sweet liqueur tasted slightly of lavender, contrasting wonderfully with the spicy gin, and giving her the kick she needed to be able to smile and say fairly normally, 'That's fine. I'm not hungry.'

'We'll have to work on getting that appetite of yours back. I was always amazed at how much you could eat.'

Melody stared at him. 'I was a dancer,' she said flatly. 'I burnt off the calories. Everything is different now.'

'Not everything.' He leant closer.

With her heart thudding, Melody waited for his kiss. As his lips closed over hers they tasted of the bittersweet cocktail and a warm thrill of pleasure quivered down her spine. When Zeke exerted his charm it was as potent as mulled wine, heady and intoxicating. He was irresistible and he knew it.

He broke the kiss for just a moment, to place their glasses on the coffee table, and then took her in his arms again, holding her lightly against him as his mouth teased at hers. She found herself swept into the world of sensuous delight Zeke evoked so easily, and as she responded to him his arms tightened around her and his lips demanded more intimacy. She abandoned all reserve—for a crazy moment she couldn't do anything else, didn't *want* to do anything else. This was Zeke and she adored him; for a few blissful seconds that was all that mattered.

It was Zeke who finished the embrace by gently withdrawing, although he still continued to hold her, his eyes as black as night as he stared down at her flushed face.

Melody felt light-headed and slightly dazed, her eyes cloudy with desire as she struggled to compose herself. Part of her was shocked and embarrassed at how easily Zeke could break through her defences; another part of her had known this would happen. Zeke was a very physical man; he'd always wanted to touch and hold and kiss her and she had wanted it too.

'You and I haven't changed,' Zeke said huskily. 'Surely you understand that now? Nothing could come between what we have. We're meant to be together. You must believe that.'

It would have been so easy to melt into him again and just agree, to let her need of him—his strength, his security, his overpowering maleness—take control. Over the past months she had been fighting constantly—fighting to get better, to control the negative thoughts that hit at all times of the night and day, to accept the fact of a future without Zeke.

Easy, but not right. That was the hard truth.

Melody stepped away from the warm circle of his arms. She looked at him and swallowed, hating what she had to say but knowing it must be said. 'It's over, Zeke,' she said, very quietly but with a finality he couldn't fail to recognise. 'I have accepted that and you *have* to. If you love me, you'll let me go. I can't be in your world any more. It might sound dramatic, but I know how much I can stand and that would be the final straw. It would destroy me here, inside. I have to make a new life for myself and find out who I am now.'

'You're my wife,' he said thickly.

If she hadn't been feeling so wretched Melody could have smiled. That was so Zeke. Black and white. He had never seen shades of grey. Not trusting herself to speak, she shook her head slowly, her eyes on his dark face.

'It's Christmas Eve.' He leant forward and kissed her again—a hard, confident kiss, strong and sweet. 'And at this moment in time you are my wife and we are going out to enjoy ourselves. We're not thinking beyond that. No more about the future, not even tomorrow. Tonight we're living in the moment, one minute at a time, and that's all that matters. Okay?'

The kiss had left her breathless and shaken, but with an effort she forced a smile. Their last night together. It was going to be bittersweet, but why couldn't it be a night to remember? A step out of time? Zeke knew how she felt, she'd made it crystal-clear, so it wasn't as if she was masquerading under false pretences. And it would be something to remember in the lonely months and years ahead.

He had retrieved their glasses and now she drank deeply of the cocktail, knowing she'd never be able to drink it again because it would be forever linked with this last night and the pain which was piercing her through.

'There's canapés and champagne waiting in our box at the theatre, so if you're ready?' Zeke said softly as she drained her glass. He took her arm, his touch firm but gentle.

Melody took a deep breath. Her first real venture into the outside world since the accident and she was certainly plunging into the deep end, she thought wryly. There was bound to be people they knew at the theatre—people who were aware of her injuries and who would be watching her with scalpel-sharp eyes. Hopefully once they were in their box there would be a degree of privacy, but until then... She squared her shoulders and lifted her chin. 'Ready.'

It was a lie. She would never be ready. And she was scared, so scared, but she could do this. It was just one night after all.

Zeke pulled her coat round her shoulders, his touch sending tiny bolts of electricity down her nerve endings. It was always the same. Even when he inadvertently touched her it registered every time.

Just before they left the room he turned her round to face him, slowly raising her left hand with her wedding and engagement rings to his lips. He kissed her wrist first, his mouth warm against the silky flesh where her pulse beat, and then turned her hand over and kissed the rings, his lips caressing and gentle. 'You've nothing to fear from me,' he said very quietly. 'I promise you that. I will never hurt you.'

She made a small ineffectual sound in her throat, pulling her hand away as she stepped back a pace.

'So defensive.' The words were almost a sigh, and for a moment she thought she detected sudden pain in his dark eyes before he blinked and it cleared.

'I thought we were leaving?' She spoke flatly, carefully keeping her facial expression calm. She couldn't afford to let her guard down. Not for a moment.

'We are.' But he didn't move.

Melody stared at him warily, swallowing against the tightness in her throat. There had always been something uncivilised about Zeke, and tonight it was in every movement and expression—a sensuousness that was almost animal-like in its instinctive earthiness and male power.

And then he smiled, opening the door. 'Let's go.'

CHAPTER SEVEN

I⊤ had stopped snowing when they left the hot-house comfort of the hotel, stepping into a frozen winter wonderland that had transformed the city streets into something magical.

The gritters had been hard at work keeping the main roads serviceable, and the hotel staff had had the foresight to clear a path from the hotel door to the main thoroughfare. Nevertheless, Melody was glad of Zeke's firm hand at her elbow as they hailed a taxi.

The snow hadn't seemed to deter the last-minute shoppers making use of some of the big stores which were still open. The white pavements were alive with folk heaped with bags and parcels, and an unusual air of gaiety pervaded the scene. It was as though a white Christmas had evoked the excitement of a child in even the most hardened city-dwellers, and for a little while the wonder of the festive season had swept away everyday problems and difficulties. Everyone seemed happy.

Zeke settled her close to him in the taxi, his arm round her shoulders, and she didn't pull away although his touch made her as tense as a coiled spring. It was strange being out in the hustle and bustle of life again after her long stint in the hospital, but it wasn't that which tightened her nerves, although he must have thought so because he murmured, 'Relax. We're doing this together, okay? I'm here. I've got you. This is going to be a pleasant evening, that's all.'

'I'm fine,' she lied firmly. 'Absolutely fine.'

The sound he made in his throat expressed what he thought of that, and as he bent and kissed the top of her head with a swift, featherlight touch she thought she heard him sigh again.

Melody stared out of the window without really seeing the brightly lit shops and crowds, overwhelmed by a mixture of emotions—fear and panic and, not least, love. His solid muscular body was against hers, filling her with the old familiar feeling of safety and belonging. When she had met Zeke she'd realised she'd been searching all her life for the security he provided. For the first time she'd felt she had a chance at the things lots of people took for granted. He would take care of her. But now that was relegated to a memory—a beautiful dream which had been sweet while it had lasted.

They didn't talk on the way to the theatre, but every so often Melody felt his lips brush the top of her head. It took all of her willpower not to twist and lift her face to his, and only the knowledge that it would be immensely unfair to give him any hope prevented her from reaching for him. She had seen sadness mingled with desire in his eyes the last time she'd met his gaze, but she knew he still hadn't accepted their marriage was over. And he had to. For both their sakes.

Zeke helped her out of the taxi once they reached the theatre, but she was still vitally conscious of her less than elegant exit, and despair at her clumsiness was paramount as she stood on the icy pavement. Mr Price had told her that she was too hard on herself more than once. 'It is the dancer in you who exaggerates what you see as ungainliness,' he'd insisted. 'Other people would not notice.'

She had blessed him for his kindness, but had known it was just that and not the truth. She had watched the smooth, controlled walk of the nurses in the hospital, of visitors, everyone, and marvelled at all she had taken for granted before the accident. But then she supposed everyone was the same in her position. She wasn't unique.

She breathed in the crisp, bitingly cold air, which due to the snow was devoid of the taint of the city for once. *Okay, best foot forward,* she told herself with silent irony as Zeke slid an arm round her waist. And they might not meet anyone they knew, anyway.

And pigs might fly!

They were barely inside the foyer when a gushing voice caused them to turn. *'Darlings...'* Angela Stewart was an actress of some standing and, Melody suspected, one of Zeke's old flames—although he had never said and she'd never asked. But there was something in the way Angela was with her made Melody feel the tall, willowy blonde resented her beneath the effusive front she presented. *'So* lovely to see you.' Angela's sharp blue eyes swept her from head to foot before the actress gave a *mwah* of a kiss to the air either side of their faces, her carefully tousled hair stiff with hairspray.

Melody braced herself. 'Hello, Angela,' she said carefully, trying to breathe through the fog of heavy perfume the blonde was wearing. Angela was the last person she'd have chosen to see.

'How *are* you?' A red-taloned hand touched Melody's arm lightly. 'We were so *devastated* when we heard about the accident, you poor, poor love. And you a dancer too. So sad.'

'She's wonderful—aren't you, sweetheart?' Zeke's

voice was cool, with an edge that made Melody hope Angela didn't prolong the conversation.

Angela's escort—a tall, distinguished man who could have doubled as Richard Gere—must have thought the same thing, because he took her arm after nodding at Melody and Zeke, saying, 'Our party's waiting to take their seats, Angela.'

Angela jerked herself free, looking straight at Melody. 'All those months in hospital must have been tedious for you. I bet you can't wait to get back in the swing of things again,' she drawled softly. 'But you must take it a day at a time, sweetie. You look a little tired and peaky.'

'Melody has the resilience of youth on her side,' Zeke put in smoothly. 'Remember how that used to feel, Angela? Now, if you'll excuse us...'

They were seated in their box before Melody spoke. 'You shouldn't have said that,' she murmured as Zeke poured the champagne which had been waiting for them. 'She'll never forgive you. I'd be surprised if she ever speaks to you again.'

Zeke grinned, offering her the plate of canapés. 'Sounds good.'

Below them the stalls were filling up, along with the balcony and the other boxes. The musical drama they were seeing was the latest big thing, and tickets were like gold dust. The theatre itself was an old building, with a high, ornate domed ceiling and an air of genteel Victorian splendour, and the central heating was equally archaic and not quite man enough for the unusually cold evening.

Like a magician producing a rabbit out of a hat, Zeke placed a thick, imitation fur throw across her legs. 'Is that better?' he murmured softly.

'Where did that come from?' Melody asked, surprised.

'I know this theatre from old. It's too hot in the summer and cold in the winter, but its charm cancels out such inconveniences.' Zeke topped up her champagne as he spoke, his voice warm as he added, 'Relax and enjoy the show. You're doing great. I'm proud of you, my darling.'

It was the look in his eyes rather than what he said that caused her to flush and gulp at her champagne. She had forgotten how he made her feel when she was with him—no, that was wrong. She bit her bottom lip. She hadn't forgotten, had merely tried to bury the memory along with a host of others. And he would never understand, not in a million years, because she didn't understand it herself. It was just this sort of thing that made it imperative she walked away from him now, while things were still civilised between them. She couldn't bear to experience a slow whittling away of such moments as their relationship went sour.

Was she crazy? She sipped her drink, staring unseeing across the theatre. Probably. Almost definitely. And certainly cowardly and weak and spineless.

She looked at him out of the corner of her eye and his dark gaze was soft on her face. 'Thinking again,' he stated ruefully. 'I would like to flick a little switch in here—' he touched her brow lightly '—and turn your head off for a while. How can I do that, my sweet wife? How can I make you live in the moment?'

She shrugged, pretending a nonchalance she didn't feel.

'I only know of one sure way, but that's impossible in here,' Zeke went on contemplatively. 'Impossible to do properly, anyway, and after waiting so long...'

Melody took another hurried sip of champagne, deciding silence was the quickest way to end this disturbing one-sided conversation. She pretended an interest in the stalls below.

'Remember how it was between us?' He stretched his long legs, sliding one arm along the back of her seat, so close his body warmth surrounded her as his quiet, smoky voice wove a deliberate spell. 'Those nights when we didn't fall asleep until dawn? The taste of pure ecstasy, long and slow and lasting. You're mine, Dee. You'll always be mine, as I'm yours. There's no other way for either of us now we've feasted on perfection.'

'Don't.' Her breath caught in her throat, his words causing a chain reaction in her body she was powerless to control. And he knew it, she thought helplessly.

'Don't?' His husky voice drifted around her like a sensuous cloud. 'Don't speak the truth? But the truth will set you free. Isn't that what they say? And you're not facing the truth. Not yet. Our lifestyle, my work, other people—that's all on the perimeter of *us*, you and me.'

He was confusing her, blurring the edges. She shook her head, on the verge of getting up and leaving. It was the dimming of the lights that forestalled such an action, but she sat stiff and taut as the show began, every nerve and sinew in her body stretched to breaking point.

In spite of her acute distress, the drama being enacted on stage began to work its magic after a while. The special effects were spellbinding, and the heroine's voice enchanting, but it was the dancers who took most of Melody's attention—especially the lead female, who was as supple and graceful as a young gazelle. It was bittersweet watching the girl, and at first pain overshadowed her perception, but then she felt herself swept into the performance to such an extent she had to bump back to earth when the interval arrived.

'Well?' Zeke's eyes were waiting for her as the lights brightened. 'Enjoying it?' he said gently.

Melody nodded, still half lost in the performance. 'It's brilliant—absolutely brilliant. And I'm not criticising, but—'

'But?' he pressed her when she stopped abruptly.

'I'd have arranged that last dance number differently. It would have been far more poignant if the lead dancer was taken by the underworld after it finished rather than pulling her out at the beginning. The scene lost something without her present.'

Zeke nodded. 'I agree.'

'That way the roles of Cassandra and Alex could have been tweaked to make them more involved in the struggle, rather than being almost observers.' Melody stopped abruptly, aware of the half-smile on Zeke's face. 'What?'

'Nothing.' Zeke turned as a waitress appeared with a plate of fresh savouries and coffee which he'd obviously arranged to have brought to their box. After tipping the girl handsomely he closed the door after her, enclosing them in their own private little world again. He solicitously plied her with the delicious morsels, and unlike previously his conversation was now easy and amusing, requiring little in response from her.

To her immense surprise Melody found she was enjoying herself in spite of the nerves still making themselves felt in the pit of her stomach. She had dreaded battling her way to the crowded bar in the interval—a place where many of their contemporaries liked to see and be seen—and with that obstacle dealt with, the pleasure of being out on the town after all her weeks incarcerated in the hospital was foremost.

Zeke handed her a cup of coffee, his thigh briefly brushing hers, and immediately she tensed. He was wearing a clean, sharp aftershave that blended well with his own personal male scent, and he had always looked exceptionally good in a dinner suit, his particular brand of hard, rugged sexiness emphasised by the formal attire. 'This is nice,' he said in a contented murmur, his brawny shoulder against hers.

It was. Too nice. Melody said nothing and the comfortable silence changed, becoming uncomfortable. Still she didn't break it. Zeke sipped his black coffee slowly, his face calm and inscrutable. She had no idea what he was thinking. Not that she ever had. The thought troubled her with its truth and she chewed it over, worrying at it like a dog with a bone.

Was it because he deliberately kept his thoughts from her and because he was enigmatic, private? Or—and here her fingers clenched on her coffee cup—because she had never taken the time to find out his innermost feelings and desires? She had been so occupied with her career, with making good, surviving in the glitzy, showy world they inhabited, that she'd been content to skate on the surface of their marriage while everything had been easy and harmonious. Her amazement that he had chosen her as his wife, that it was all too good to be true, had induced a feeling that she must be careful not to rock the boat and it had been simpler not to delve too deeply.

Children, for instance. She glanced at his chiselled profile, her heart thudding. When they'd spoken of a family she had sensed he wanted children soon, but she'd never really talked to him about that, preferring to relegate it to somewhere in the hazy future. From the way he'd spoken earlier, when the two little Japanese girls had prompted things, it was clear he wanted to be a father—probably needed to create a family unit more than most men due to his upbringing. He would want to give his own children everything he'd never had. Why had she never realised that before?

Because she hadn't taken the time to consider; she had been too busy keeping up with how she felt the wife of Zeke James should be. It symbolised everything which had been wrong in their relationship before the accident and most of it was down to her. But it had been impossible to bring her insecurities into the open because they'd been buried too deep, locked way in the small, scared child part of herself. But she wasn't a child any more. She was a grown woman, and she had to come to terms with her buried fears and emotions before she could function properly as a person, let alone a wife.

She was a mess. Melody sipped at her coffee as tears pricked the backs of her eyes. Zeke didn't deserve to be landed with a nutcase like her. He wouldn't divorce her. He'd made his commitment and he would never go back on it—that was the sort of man he was. So it was up to her to end things and let him find happiness in the future with someone who was his equal—something she'd never felt from day one.

When his hand moved her face to look at him she was too late to blink away the tears. He surveyed her steadily, his black eyes velvet-soft, but the solid strength that had first attracted her was very evident. 'It will be all right.' His thumbs brushed away the telltale moisture. 'Now you're back with me everything will slot into place, you'll see.'

She shook her head very slightly. 'No, Zeke. It won't.'

He looked at her gravely. 'Do you seriously think your scars will have any impact on my love for you? Apart from increasing my admiration for the way you've fought to overcome your injuries? Just how shallow do you think I am?'

'I don't think you're shallow.' She swallowed hard. 'And I've come to realise this is about me, not you. I should never have married you. I shouldn't have married anyone—not until I knew myself. Not until I understood where my problems were.'

His face was expressionless. 'And do you know yourself now?'

'I'm beginning to.' She moistened dry lips. 'And I didn't realise what a headcase I was.'

'No, not a headcase.' His voice was calm, level. 'Merely vulnerable and afraid and unconfident. You have always been those things, Dee. This is no surprise to me. You are also courageous and sweet and generous, with the softest heart of anyone I have ever known. The positives outweigh the negatives big time. If you're going to examine yourself, do it properly.'

She stiffened a little. 'You think you know me so well?'

'I know I do.' His smile was almost pensive.

'You're very sure of yourself, aren't you?'

'I have to be,' he said quietly. 'For your sake as well as mine. The accident has brought to the surface issues which would have been dealt with slowly, over a matter of years, if it hadn't happened. But it has happened. And maybe it's for the best.'

She stared at him, hurt beyond measure. 'How can you say that?' she accused thickly, the physical and mental agony she'd suffered over the past months rising up in a bitter flood. 'I've lost everything I've worked for all my life.'

His face tightened, but his voice was still calm and controlled when he said, 'No, Dee. You have lost the ability to dance as you once did. That has been taken away from you. But that's all. You can still see and hear and smell and touch. Your mind hasn't been damaged, your intellect is still as sharp, and you can make decisions about where you want to go and what you want to do and carry them out without being dependent on others to enable you to move or walk. There are plenty of people—some of them in that hospital you've just left—who would give ten years of their lives for that alone. You have everything to live for.'

Anger replaced the hurt. 'You're accusing me of self-pity?'

He looked at her intently with those ebony-dark eyes. 'Your words, not mine,' he said quietly as the lights began to dim once more. He settled back in his seat, his face inscrutable.

Melody barely heard the orchestra strike up. She sat staring towards the stage, fighting hot, angry tears and telling herself she hated him. *Hated* him. How dared he say all that to her after all she had been through? Didn't he understand how this had changed her life? Didn't he care? She had been right to insist on a divorce—this proved it.

The curtain rose, but it was a few minutes before she focused on the drama being enacted on the stage. The drama in her own life was paramount. She could feel Zeke's eyes on her now and then as the musical progressed, but she didn't glance at him once.

The anger and outrage subsided after a while, and a quiet but insistent little voice deep inside was telling her that Zeke was right. Right, but cruel and hard and unfeeling, she told herself bitterly. How could he say he loved her and talk to her like that?

It was another twenty minutes before she could bring herself to acknowledge that Zeke had said what no one else would dare to say, because he felt she needed to hear it. In all the time she had known him she had never seen him be anything but ruthlessly honest and direct. It was just that the searing truthfulness had never been directed at her before—or not with such severity, anyway. Nevertheless, if this was tough love she didn't want it.

By the time the last curtain call was finished, to rapturous applause from a very satisfied audience, Melody felt like a wet rag. If she had just endured twenty sessions with a therapist without a break she couldn't have been more exhausted or emotionally drained, she thought, as the lights rose and people began to stand up. It was as though in the past few hours since leaving hospital the door in her mind where all her insecurities and issues had been under lock and key had been flung wide open, and she was having to deal with the resulting cans of worms in one fell swoop. Some Christmas Eve, she thought wretchedly.

She must have looked as spent as she felt, because Zeke's voice was genuinely concerned when he said, 'We can skip dinner out and order Room Service when we get back to the hotel, if you would prefer that? It's probably more sensible with the weather.'

Melody nodded. The thought of an intimate twosome was scary, but she got clumsy when she was tired, and anything was preferable than falling flat on her face in every sense of the words. 'If that's okay?'

He kissed her, a slow, gentle kiss, and she didn't have

the energy to protest. 'Come on,' he said softly. 'Let's go home.'

If only they were, Melody thought suddenly, swallowing at the constriction in her throat. If only this was a year ago, when everything had been all right. But *had* it been? Really?

She was stiff when she rose from her seat, and concentrating on walking as best she could helped to quell the lump in her throat. They had barely left the box when Zeke drew her into his arms and kissed her again. It was a very confident kiss, strong and sweet, and his fingers massaged the base of her spine as his mouth worked its magic. He didn't hurry. He took his time.

Melody felt breathless and shaken when his mouth left hers, and his eyes were smiling as they stared down into her wide green ones. 'My brand of physiotherapy,' he said smokily, his features shadowed in the dim light in the corridor in which they were standing. 'And it's very exclusive.'

A thrill of unexpected laughter went through her. 'Have you been qualified for long?' she murmured.

'I'm a novice,' he admitted softly. 'I need a lot of practice.' His finger outlined her lips. 'Practice makes perfect. Isn't that what they say?'

Her mouth went dry. With an effort she held the smile. 'Whoever "they" are, I'm sure they've got a point.' She extracted herself from his arms. 'We'll be the last ones out of the theatre if we're not careful.'

Zeke grinned. 'Suits me.'

It suited her too. The last thing she wanted to do tonight was make polite conversation with any more Angelas. The trouble with Zeke being so high-profile was that wherever they went he was recognised by someone or other. Not that he could help that. And it didn't matter—or it hadn't mattered much in the past, anyway. It was different now.

'I don't like being the last at anything,' she said, determined not to get embroiled in another weakening embrace, and when Zeke took her arm without another word and led her to the stairs she knew he had taken her none too subtle hint.

The taxi Zeke had booked to take them to their dinner venue was waiting when they walked out of the theatre, the icy cold taking Melody's breath away. Enclosed in the cosy cocoon of their box, she had forgotten the sub-zero temperature outside for an hour or two. He drew her firmly into him as they walked across the pavement, helping her into the taxi and giving the driver their new destination before settling beside her. He slid his arm along the seat at the back of her, a familiar action—and why it should result in her heart hammering in wild, panicked beats she didn't know. She was too weary and emotionally spent to protest when he drew her head onto his shoulder, besides which it was achingly familiar.

'Christmas Eve,' he murmured above her head, his voice soft. 'Your favourite night. The night of miracles.'

So he'd remembered. She had told him the first Christmas they had been together that Christmas Eve had always been special to her in some way she couldn't explain. All through her lonely childhood and even lonelier teenage years the day had held an elusive wonder her circumstances couldn't dispel or negate. It seemed a time for miracles, the restoration of lost dreams and hopes and aspirations, and she had never ceased to be affected by it.

Except for tonight. The thought pierced her through, but it was true. Tonight she was bowed down by reality and she had nothing to look forward to—no expectancy or belief that there was a ray of light at the end of her particular dark tunnel. She simply didn't have it in her to trust she wouldn't spoil what they had if she stayed with Zeke. She couldn't live with the doubt and uncertainty, the wondering, the fear it would turn sour and he'd be driven into someone else's arms. Someone with beauty and grace who was whole and happy and unscathed by life. A girl who could return his love with all her heart and trust him implicitly.

This was going to be their last night together. She nodded mentally to the thought. Somehow she would slip away tomorrow, find somewhere—anywhere—to stay. She had one or two friends who lived in this area. One of them would take her in. It wasn't the best time to turn up on someone's doorstep—Christmas Day—but she couldn't help that. She had to escape Zeke. She had to make him *see*. Zeke wasn't for her. And she didn't believe in miracles any more.

CHAPTER EIGHT

AMAZINGLY, in view of her misery, Melody must have fallen asleep, because the next thing she knew was the taxi stopping and Zeke's voice saying they were back at the hotel.

'Come on, sleepyhead.' His voice was tender, indulgent, as he helped her out of the car. 'How about you change into something comfortable when we get to the suite? Maybe have a warm bath first? It'll take Room Service a while to deliver once we've ordered so you'll have plenty of time.'

She glanced at him as they walked into the foyer, knowing her limp was more pronounced tonight but unable to do anything about it. 'I think I'll go straight to my room,' she said tightly. 'And I'm not hungry. I'll skip dinner, if you don't mind.'

'Hungry or not, you need to eat.'

'No, Zeke. I don't. I told you—I'm going straight to bed.'

They had reached the lift, and once the doors closed he faced her in the carpeted little box, his voice dangerously soft. 'Dinner is compulsory, Dee. Unless you want me to choose for you, I suggest you look at the menu.'

'For goodness' sake.' Truly exasperated, she glared

at him. 'What are you going to do? Force-feed me?' she said irritably.

'If necessary.' He nodded. 'Exactly that.'

She could see he wasn't joking. 'I'm not a child, Zeke.'

'Then don't act like one. You have been seriously ill and you're still recovering. You need good food and plenty of it.'

This was ridiculous. 'I think I'm quite capable of knowing when I want to eat, thank you very much,' she said tartly.

Zeke raised his eyebrows as a smile flickered across his sexy mouth. The action said far more than words could have done and aggravated her further. Did he have to be so irritatingly chauvinistic? Melody thought waspily. And so certain he was always right?

She gave him what she hoped was a quelling glare and stared at the lift door as though it was the most interesting thing on the planet, knowing it was useless to argue. Nevertheless she was bristling like a furious little alley cat, determined not to give ground, when they opened the door to their suite. Whether Zeke was right or wrong didn't matter. It was his peremptory attitude that had got under her skin.

The lights from the Christmas tree and the couple of lamps Zeke had left on made the sitting room dangerously cosy as they took off their coats—a miniature home from home. Zeke slung his jacket on a chair, loosening his bow tie and opening the first two or three buttons of his shirt as he walked across to the coffee table where the room service menu was sitting. 'Now,' he murmured smoothly. 'I think the steak will do me nicely. How about you? And the raspberry and limoncello trifle sounds good. I'm starving.'

Melody plumped down sulkily on one of the sofas. She wouldn't have admitted to a living soul that her mouth had watered as he spoke. 'I had beef for lunch,' she said stiffly.

'How about oven-poached salmon with fennel and beetroot?' Zeke suggested amiably. 'That's a light alternative and not so rich as most of the other dishes. Perfect to tempt the appetite.'

She shrugged, knowing she was acting like the child he had accused her of being but not knowing how else to protect herself against the temptation he presented. He looked more hard and sexy than any man had the right to look, and his lazy air and lack of aggression didn't fool her one bit. 'I think I will have a bath,' she said flatly, as Zeke picked up the telephone, leaving the room without waiting for him to reply.

Once in her bedroom she shut the door and leaned her weight against it, wondering for the umpteenth time how she had got herself into this situation. 'It's just one night,' she whispered. 'Nothing has really changed.' Her plans hadn't altered, and Zeke couldn't keep her married to him by force when all was said and done. She just had to keep her head and by this time tomorrow she could be somewhere else—*anywhere* else. Her soft mouth dropped unknowingly and she levered herself upright with a shuddering sigh.

She wanted to be a million miles away from Zeke, and yet she longed to be where she could see and watch and touch him every minute of every day. How was that for inconsistency? And she couldn't let him see or even sense what she was feeling. She was no match for him at the best of times and his formidably intelligent mind and finely honed senses—attributes which had caused him to rise like a meteor in the world he inhabited—were at their most astute when concentrated on a problem he needed to solve. And at the moment she had no doubt that was how he viewed this situation. He hadn't even begun to accept their marriage was over, everything about him proclaimed it, and so she had to remain strong and focused.

Melody didn't linger in the bath, drying herself thoroughly and slipping into a pyjama vest top and matching loose trousers and then pulling on the fluffy bathrobe for added protection. She hadn't heard a sound from outside her room but as she opened the bedroom door she could hear carols being sung. A carol concert was in full swing on the TV as she entered the sitting room, young choir boys singing 'Silent Night' with a purity of tone that was inexpressibly poignant.

Zeke was sprawled on one of the sofas, his long legs stretched out in front of him and a glass of brandy at his elbow. He looked broodingly tough and fascinatingly sexy, and Melody's mouth went dry at the sight of him. His eyes opened as she walked into the room and he straightened slightly, indicating his drink with a wave of his hand. 'Like one?'

She shook her head. 'I've had more than enough today, thanks,' she said, pleased her voice sounded so normal when her heart was pounding like a drum. 'I haven't had any alcohol for the last three months, don't forget.'

'I haven't forgotten one second of the last three months, believe me. The time's engraved on my memory for ever. Sheer hell.'

He had moved so she could join him on the sofa but she deliberately sat facing him on the opposite one, pretending an interest in the cathedral where the concert was being filmed as she tucked her feet under her legs, curling up and pulling the robe over her toes. 'It's very beautiful,' she said quietly. 'There's a timeless quality to such places, isn't there?'

'Why have you shut me out so completely?' His voice wasn't accusing, in fact it was verging on conversational, and for a moment the words didn't register. 'I mean, I'd really like to know.'

'Zeke, please don't start this again. It's no good.'

'For such a soft, gentle creature you can be as hard as iron when you want to be,' he said thoughtfully.

Stung, she met his gaze. 'I'm not hard.'

'Not with the rest of the world, no. Just with me. Why is that? What is it about me that makes you believe I don't bleed when I'm cut? That I don't feel like other people?'

She drew in a deep breath. 'I know the last months have been hard for you too. I do know that. But that doesn't make any difference to now.'

'Do you blame me for the fact I wasn't with you when it happened?' he asked quietly. 'That's completely understandable. I hold myself responsible. I could have—should have—prevented it. I let you down and it's unforgivable.'

Shocked beyond measure, she stared at him. 'Of course I don't blame you. How could I?'

'Very easily,' he said flatly, leaning forward so his hands were clasped between his knees, his dark gaze tight on her pale face. 'We were supposed to meet for lunch that day. I would have been with you but for that problem that arose. If I hadn't cancelled, put a damn business meeting before my wife—'

'Stop it, Zeke,' she whispered, horrified. 'The accident was nothing to do with you. It was me. For a brief moment of time I didn't think. It's as simple as that.

Probably countless thousands of people have momentary lapses of concentration every day. I was just in the wrong place at the wrong time to have mine. But it wasn't your fault.'

She had forgotten they'd been supposed to meet at a little bistro that day, before he had called and made his apologies; the trauma of the accident and the following days and nights of unconsciousness had wiped it from her mind. But even if she had remembered she would never have imagined he blamed himself for what had happened. Zeke was such a logical man—so rational and clear-headed. She couldn't believe he had been condemning himself all this time. The fault had been hers and hers alone.

He stood restlessly to his feet, shaking his head. 'I don't see it that way but we won't argue about it.' His eyes held hers. 'I'm not going to let you go, Dee. Not after nearly losing you three months ago.'

It was the hardest thing she had ever done in her life to look back at him and speak the painful truth. 'You have no choice. It takes two to make a partnership and I can't do it any more. I need...' She paused, knowing her voice was shaking but unable to keep the tremours from showing. 'I *want* a divorce, Zeke. Our lives are set to go down different paths now. Surely you see that as much as I do? We can't go back to the way things were. It's over.'

Two small words that cut like a knife through all the intimacy they had shared, the good times, the laughter, the joy and pleasure. She watched his face change, becoming set and rigid, as though he'd pulled a mask into place hiding any emotion. 'And what I want and feel counts for nothing?'

Melody unconsciously gripped her hands together,

struggling for composure. 'I'm doing this for you as well as me—'

'Don't give me that.' He didn't shout, but the tone of his voice stopped her mid-sentence. 'That's too easy a get-out and you know it. Never once today have you asked me what I want or how I'm feeling. You've simply stated you're walking and that's that. No discussion, no compromise, no nothing.'

She could see why it appeared that way to him, but how could she explain it was sheer self-survival driving her? She had always felt out of her depth in Zeke's world, but before the accident she had known she was out of the ordinary in one way—her dancing. She was good, more than good, and it had been the foundation of who she was—for right or wrong. Now that foundation was gone, smashed by a ten-ton truck…

The ball of pain in her stomach that had nothing to do with her accident and all to do with leaving Zeke contracted suddenly, as though a steel fist had been driven deep into her solar plexus. Without picking her words, she whispered, 'When I was a little girl I was always on the outside looking in. I didn't get invited to parties or to tea with anyone. No one waited to walk home from school with me or called for me at the weekends to go to the park or play at their house. Of course looking back now I know it was because my grandmother never let me have friends round and she wasn't friendly with the other mothers, but then I thought it was me. That the other girls didn't like *me*—thought me odd because I hadn't got a mother and father like them. Perhaps they did or didn't. I don't know. But then I found that when I danced the rest of the world didn't matter. I lost myself. I wasn't me any more. And my grandmother encouraged it, knowing how much it meant to me. She did do that for me.'

'While effectively screwing you up in every other way.'

Taken aback by the bitterness and outrage in his voice, Melody shook her head quickly. 'No, no she didn't. She—she did the best she could—the same as we all do, I suppose. She didn't have to take me in, she could have let me go into care, but she didn't. And she had been hurt—badly. I think she loved my grandfather very much, and certainly she never got over him. Her way of dealing with it was to hide her pain behind a façade of being tough. And she had lost her daughter too—my mother. She had a lot to cope with.'

'You're making excuses for her. You always do,' he said softly, the harshness gone from his voice.

'I'm trying to explain.' The unexplainable. And opening up like this terrified her. But he deserved this at least.

'Dee, you're more than a dancer. You've always been more than a dancer.' He'd come and crouched in front of her as he spoke, his trousers stretched tight over muscled thighs.

The temperature in the room rose about twenty degrees and all coherent thought went out of Melody's head. She stared at him, knowing he was going to kiss her and wanting it more than she had wanted anything in her life.

The polite knock at the door to the suite followed by a male voice calling, 'Room Service,' came as a drenching shock. Zeke reacted before she did, standing up and walking across the room while Melody made a heroic effort to pull herself together.

The man bustled in with a laden serving trolley,

quickly and efficiently setting the small table in a corner of the room with cutlery and napkins, lighting the two candles in a silver candelabrum which he'd brought with him and placing it in the centre of the table. 'Would you like me to serve the food, sir?' he asked Zeke, after he'd opened the bottle of wine Zeke had obviously ordered and offered him a taste before pouring a little into two large wine glasses.

Zeke glanced across at Melody, who was still sitting on the sofa. 'No, we'll be fine. Thank you, and happy Christmas.'

He slipped the man a tip which made the waiter's, 'And a very merry Christmas to you, sir, madam,' positively euphoric as he left, and as Melody joined him at the table Zeke pulled out a chair, unfolding her napkin and placing it in her lap as she sat down. 'May I serve the first course, madam?'

Lifting the covers off two delicate white-and-silver bowls, he revealed creamy, steaming soup which smelt divine. 'I didn't order this.' Melody glanced into his dark face.

'I thought we'd do it properly.' He slid a fresh crusty roll onto a small plate next to her soup and then took his own place at the table. 'Eat,' he ordered softly.

The soup was as delicious as it smelt, and the salmon which followed equally good. Zeke talked of inconsequential matters with a comfortable ease which relaxed Melody in spite of herself, teasing her a little and making her laugh, his humour gentle and self-deprecating. Lulled into a mellow state of mind by Zeke's lazy air, the light yet satisfying food and the wine she sipped almost unconsciously, Melody found herself drifting in a haze of well-being. She felt calm and peaceful inside, she realised with a little shock of self-awareness. For the first time in months. It was such an alien sensation.

By the time Zeke brought out the desserts Melody was sure she couldn't eat another thing, but the Madeira cake spread with lemon curd, dosed with limoncello liqueur and topped off with raspberries and a mascarpone custard was the perfect end to a perfect meal and she ate every morsel. Replete, she finished the last of her wine, and when Zeke got up from the table and pulled her over to one of the sofas, sitting down beside her, she didn't protest.

'It's midnight,' he murmured after a moment or two, his voice smoky-soft. 'Happy Christmas, darling.'

Darling. He shouldn't call her darling, she thought, but then she pushed the reasoning behind it away, not wanting anything to intrude on the moment. She watched as he reached into his pocket, bringing out a small package which he handed her, kissing her once very lightly. 'What is it?' she said suspiciously.

'Open it and see.'

'Zeke, I didn't want anything—'

'Shush.' His mouth was harder, more insistent, and this time the kiss left her entire body trembling when he raised his head. 'Open it,' he said again, his voice husky.

The eternity ring was exquisite: sparkling diamonds and emeralds set into a delicate ring of white gold. When Zeke slid it onto her finger it nestled perfectly between her wedding ring and engagement ring, which was a beautiful thing in itself, with emeralds clustered round a magnificent diamond. Melody stared down at the glittering stones, anguish vying with other emotions she couldn't even bring a name to. She pressed the palms of her hands onto her eyes, hating herself for what she was doing to him.

Zeke gently brought her fingers away from her face by grasping her wrists, his dark eyes gazing into her tormented ones when she stared at him. He had aged in the past three months, she realised with a little shock of mortification. Time had become ingrained in the features of his face, the way it did when someone had suffered unbearable bereavement or loss. Had he unconsciously let go of her? In some deep recess of his mind had he known what they'd had was over? Was that it? Knowing Zeke as she did, he would have fought such a feeling. He would have felt he was letting her down.

'I love you,' he said simply. 'That's all this means. I will always love you. This feeling isn't optional. It's not something I can turn on and off. When you came into my life I thought I was doing all right, that I was autonomous, cool—call it what you will. Your arrival was unexpected and unsolicited. I wasn't looking for for ever. I don't think I even understood the notion until you stood on that stage and danced your way into my heart.'

Her breath caught in her throat. 'I can't dance any more.'

'But you are here. That's all that matters.' He lowered his head until their lips were millimetres apart. 'You have to believe that, Dee, because I don't know how to convince you beyond saying it and showing you how much I love you.'

With a soft exhalation she accepted his mouth on hers. She fell against him, needing his strength, his maleness, his overwhelming virility, all the qualities she'd missed so deeply. He kissed her heavy eyelids, one after the other, pressing them closed as though he knew she needed to shut everything but the feel and taste of him out of her mind. Melody found herself in a velvety darkness made up entirely of what his body was doing to hers, her desire mounting as he deliberately deepened the kiss until the reality of the touch and taste and smell of him was irresistible, a fire which burnt everything in its path. She wanted him. She ached with it.

He picked her up in his arms, carrying her towards his bedroom. He manoeuvred the door open and carried her over the threshold as gently as if she were a china figurine. Kicking the door shut behind him, he walked into the dark bedroom, lit only by the soft shadowed glow of a bedside lamp he must have left on earlier.

Melody tensed as he laid her down on the bed, but instantly he was beside her, wrapping his arms round her in a gesture intended to reassure and comfort. There was no force, no urgency, his mouth caressing her lips with small kisses that gave pleasure without demanding a response.

Her breasts were pressed against the hard wall of his chest, and slowly and repetitively Zeke began stroking her back, his mouth moving all over her face in the same swift kisses as his fingers carefully worked down her spine from her tense shoulders to the seductive flare of her hips. Gradually she relaxed again, her body curving into his as his lips returned to her mouth and he kissed her more deeply, his skilful hands and mouth evoking the burning desire she remembered from the past.

When he removed the robe she was barely aware of it, and then he pulled the pyjama top over her head, caressing the silky skin of her throat and shoulders and nuzzling at the hollow of her collarbone before kissing her breasts one by one. She moaned deep in her throat when his mouth seized one nipple, giving it exquisite

attention before moving to the other, and now her hands
moved feverishly over his flesh, pulling the shirt away
from his body so she could run her fingers over the
hair-roughened muscle rippling with each movement
he made.

Her mouth moved where her fingers had explored,
her tongue curling round a copper nipple that beaded at
her touch. She could taste a faint saltiness on his skin,
the smell of lemon from the soap he used mingling with
a more earthy scent. She had told him once in the early
days of their marriage that she thought he was beautiful and he'd laughed, saying only women were beautiful. But he was wrong. He *was* beautiful, his body as
powerful and perfectly honed as the statues of the old
Greek gods that graced Mount Olympus.

'I've missed this,' he murmured huskily. 'Not neces-
sarily the sex but being able to hold you, to know that
you're there, that I only have to stretch out my hand to
touch you.'

She knew what he meant. There were some things
more intimate than the act of intercourse—small actions between a couple that spoke of a relationship, of
sharing, of being committed.

'Mind you, sex is great,' he added in a hoarse whisper as her hand felt for his arousal, finding the taut flesh
between his legs and stroking it. 'I'm not advocating
celibacy.'

The dark shadows gave her the confidence to flow
with what was happening, and when he removed her
pyjama bottoms and the rest of his own clothes her arms
reached for him, pulling him on top of her. She wasn't
allowing herself to think. If she thought her conscience
would force her to stop this, unfair on him as it was,

because this one night wouldn't change anything. And so she didn't think. She just felt and touched and tasted.

Now he was naked her hand circled and caressed his huge erection again, knowing she was inflicting a pleasure-pain as he groaned and caught her wrist. 'We're going to take this slow and easy,' he breathed raggedly. 'We've waited too long to rush things, but I'm only human, Dee.'

His eyes glittered like an animal's in the near darkness, his face planes and hollows, and she reached up and placed her palms along either side of his face. Although he had shaved earlier the stubble already coming through gave his skin a rough, sandpapery texture that was at odds with the boyish quiff falling across his forehead. 'Tonight it's just me and you,' she whispered breathlessly. 'No past, no future, just the present. I want to make love to you, Zeke. I want to feel you inside me again.'

'Not as much as I want to be there.' He kissed her again, a kiss she more than matched, but when she tried to guide him into her again he removed her hand. 'Later,' he murmured. 'We have all the time in the world.'

He began to touch and taste every inch of her body, teasing her with a slow sensuality that had her mindless and panting beneath his ministrations. Her skin became sensitised all over, the feminine core of her throbbing and swelling as she twisted and quivered under his mouth and hands.

Their lovemaking was as good as it had ever been, and the feelings were the same, but different. Before she had imagined they knew all there was to know about each other. Now she felt she didn't know herself, let alone Zeke. But one thing she was sure about was that she wanted him, and she wanted him because she loved him. She would always love him. She knew that now. It was part of what had terrified her after the accident. Maybe deep inside it had always terrified her. Love gave the beloved such power, such control. It had broken her grandmother, probably her mother too, and it would break her if she stayed and let it happen.

And then all reasoning became blurred again as desire took over—a desire only Zeke could quench. He moved slightly and she felt the tip of his masculinity at the mound between her thighs. He moved again and entered her just the tiniest bit, causing her legs to wrap round him as her body urged him closer and she arched her hips.

His mouth found hers once more, his lips warm and firm, and as his tongue thrust a path into her inner sweetness he possessed her to the full, the sensation extremely satisfying. He waited one moment, while her body adjusted to the swollen hardness of him, and then began to thrust strongly, building their shared excitement as the pleasure became almost unbearable in its intensity.

When the moment of climax came Melody thought she would shatter into a million pieces, her muscles contracting so violently that Zeke reached his peak a second later, his body shuddering as he groaned her name. And when the pulsing of their flesh quietened he collapsed on top of her, burying his face in the curve of her throat as he murmured her name again, his voice tender and soft.

It was a while before he half lifted himself on one elbow, studying her flushed face as he said lazily, 'Wow. If this is what a period of abstinence does, it's not all bad.' He smoothed a lock of hair from one cheek, his tough light. 'You're something else, woman.'

'You're not so bad yourself,' she managed fairly normally, thankful his mood was so relaxed and light-hearted. She couldn't have handled any more soul-searching right at this moment. A part of her knew that Zeke would see their making love as a means of putting everything right between them, but she would deal with that when she had to.

He pulled the duvet over them both, tucking her against him with his arm round her shoulders. 'How can even a hotel room become home when you're with the person you love, whereas our house was just bricks and mortar with you gone? It's made me realise I could live in a mud hut and be perfectly happy if you were there.'

Melody forced a creditable laugh. 'I can't see you in a mud hut—not unless it was fitted with internet access and enough mod-cons to let you keep your finger on the pulse.'

There was a moment of vibrating silence before Zeke shifted, lifting her chin so he could meet her eyes. 'Is that so?' he said lazily. 'If someone heard that who didn't know me they'd think I was a control freak.'

She never had known when he was joking, and she didn't now. She looked at him for several long seconds before she saw the twinkle in his eye. 'Oh, you,' she murmured weakly, snuggling into the side of him.

'Actually, you've got me all wrong.' He kissed the top of her head, his voice rumbling deep inside his chest where she pressed her face against his torso. 'Like I said to you before, my work doesn't control me. It never has. I do what I do because I enjoy it and because it has been fulfilling on the whole. Sometimes a situation has gripped me and I've put too much effort in for too little reward, but not often. Other times I've made mistakes. Like the time I cancelled a certain luncheon engagement because of a crisis that I thought only I could solve. Biggest mistake of my life.'

He paused, his voice wry when he said, 'Maybe there has been a touch of control freak there after all, but no more.'

A leopard couldn't change its spots, and why should Zeke change, anyway? She had known what she was getting into when she'd married him after all. But things had been different then. She had been different. And she couldn't go back to how she'd been.

Suddenly all the reasons why it had been madness to sleep with him again were there, panic coursing through her as she realised what she'd done. She wasn't aware that she had tensed or changed her position in any way, but she must have done, because his voice was deep and expressionless when he said, 'What's the matter? You're retreating again.'

She wriggled out of his arms, swinging her legs over the side of the bed as she said, 'Don't be silly. I—I need the bathroom.' She looked for her pyjamas, but the items of clothing scattered on the floor all looked the same in the shadows. The thought of walking to the *en-suite* naked was unthinkable. What if he put the main lights on or followed her? But she couldn't sit there all night. The thoughts flowed with the swiftness of terror. And if she started scrabbling about for her pyjamas she'd look ridiculous.

'Dee?' He touched her back and she flinched. 'Have I said something? I was trying to be honest.'

'It's fine.' Even to herself her voice sounded brittle. Knowing she had to do something, and fast, she stood up and practically ran to his bathroom, shutting the door behind her and leaning against it for a moment before grabbing the white towelling hotel robe from the back of it and sliding it on. Jerking the belt tight, she shut her eyes in relief, her breath expelling in a deep sigh. She was safe. He hadn't seen her.

She had known Zeke would follow. When a tap came at the door her eyes opened. 'Dee? Are you okay?' he called softly.

She pulled the belt tighter. 'Yes, I'm fine.'

'I don't believe you.' His voice was strained.

'I'm all right, I promise. I just need a minute, that's all. Please, Zeke. I'll be out in a moment.'

There was a pause, and she could almost hear his mind whirring. Then his voice came quiet and steady. 'I'll get us a drink. What would you like? Wine? Fruit juice? Or coffee, tea, hot chocolate? There's plenty in the fridge as well as hot drinks.'

Numbly, she forced her lips to move. 'A coffee. Thanks.'

'Don't be long.' A pause. 'I miss you already.'

She waited until she was sure he'd gone and then turned on the light, staring at her reflection in the mirror over the wash basin. A wild-eyed, pale-faced woman stared back at her and she barely recognised herself in the haunted features.

What had she done? *What had she done?* And what sort of message had sleeping with him sent to Zeke? No, Zeke, I don't want to stay married to you. Oh, yes, Zeke, you can take me to bed. No, Zeke, there's no future for us. Oh, yes, Zeke, the more intimate we are the better.

She sat down on the edge of the bath, her fingers pressing tight into her closed eyelids as though she could shut out the memory of the past hour, erase it from her mind by an iron will. But of course that was impossible. She'd done some stupid things in her life but this went far beyond stupid. Infinitely beyond. It was cruel and selfish and unreasonable and totally unforgivable. He would hate her now and she didn't blame him.

She was still berating herself when another tap came at the door. Zeke's voice was light, with a thread of steel. 'If you don't come out, I'm coming in.'

Her hands tightened on the edge of the bath and then she stood up, opening the door. 'I was just coming.'

'I thought you'd prefer coffee in the sitting room,' Zeke said coolly. He was wearing the black silk pyjama bottoms and nothing else, and he looked hard and tough and sexy, his hair ruffled and his eyes ebony-dark as they scoured her face. 'And then perhaps you can tell me why you left our bed like a scalded cat. I was under the mistaken impression it'd been great.'

His words caught her on the raw, but at least the dose of adrenaline provided the strength she needed to face him. 'Firstly, it's not our bed. It's yours,' she pointed out, sailing past him and making her way into the sitting room. 'Secondly, I did not leave like a scalded cat or a scalded anything.'

She glanced at the coffee table, where coffee and a plate of biscuits were waiting, a sofa pulled close, and then walked across to the window, opening the curtains and looking out. It was snowing again—beautiful, starry flakes that whirled and danced as though they were enjoying their brief life to the full.

She was aware of Zeke coming up behind her and then his arms enclosed her. Her back rested against his chest and his chin nuzzled her hair. 'Okay, let's have it,' he said softly. 'I've got the message that all is not yet resolved.'

She didn't know how to say it. 'I—I don't want you to get the wrong idea,' she said lamely, hating herself.

'Lady, I don't know if I'm on foot or horseback,' he drawled with dark amusement, 'so the wrong idea's the least of it. That *was* you I made love with a while ago, wasn't it? You haven't got a clone who doubles for you now and again?'

'What I mean is—'

'What you mean,' he interrupted, turning her round to face him but still keeping her in the circle of his arms, 'is that in spite of having your wicked way with me you are still holding to this ridiculous notion of a divorce. Correct?'

She couldn't tell if he was furious and hiding it extremely well, or if the slightly sardonic attitude was for real. Zeke was a master of the inscrutable. Warily, she nodded.

'Okay. So you've got that off your chest. Drink your coffee.'

He had to take this seriously. 'Zeke, you have to understand—'

He stopped her with a breath-stealing kiss. 'Come and have your coffee and biscuits. And then we're going to talk some. We should probably have talked before we finished up in the bedroom, but I never did profess to be perfect.'

'There's nothing to say,' she protested helplessly.

'There's plenty. Let me put it this way, Dee. Until you can convince me it's over, it's not over.'

Melody stiffened in defence of his arrogance, her hands pushing against the wall of his chest. 'Let me go.'

'Sure.' She was free immediately. 'But you still have

to convince me. You're part of me, Dee. One half of the whole. I have certain rights. You married me, remember?'

'You talk as if you own me.' She was shaking inside, his closeness a sweet torment, but she knew if she didn't attack she would be lost. 'Do you know that? Is that what you believe?'

'Only in as much as you own me,' he said softly. 'It works both ways. You gave me your love and so that's mine—as my love is yours. The difference between us is that I trust you. I trust you with everything I am and everything I have. But you're not there yet, are you? There's still a question mark hanging over my head like the sword of Damocles. True trust involves commitment, becoming vulnerable, Dee. It can make you feel exposed and frightened. Oh, yes, it can. Don't look at me like that. Do you think you're the only one who's scared rigid at the enormity of what true love and trust involves? But it's worth it. In the long run, it's worth it.'

She shook her head, unaware of the tears coursing down her face until he stepped forward and stroked the moisture away with his fingers. 'It's going to be okay,' he reassured her very quietly, his eyes dark and steady. 'You're a good person and so am I. In fact I'm a great person. We're destined to be together.'

It was so silly that she had to smile, as he'd meant her to. 'I don't want to hurt you,' she whispered, in such a low voice he could barely hear her, 'but better that now than later. This—us—it's impossible, Zeke.'

He drew her over to the sofa, pushing her down and handing her a coffee made from the complementary tray left in the room. 'This is your night.' He put a biscuit in the saucer of her cup. 'A night that laughs at the impossible. Only believe.'

That was just it. She couldn't. Melody put the cup to her lips, not even noticing the milk was the long-life sort that she hated. She couldn't believe any more.

CHAPTER NINE

THEY sipped their coffee in silence, eating the biscuits automatically. Melody didn't want to talk and start the process of discussion again. There was nothing more to be said. She was so tired—not the physical, bone-weary kind she'd experienced earlier, but tired in her spirit. Arguments and counter-arguments—she had been going over them in her head for weeks alone in her hospital bed. There was nothing new Zeke could say that she hadn't already considered. She was all reasoned out.

'Let's go and build a snowman.'

If Zeke had said *Let's take a trip to the moon tonight,* Melody couldn't have stared at him with more amazement. 'What?'

'A snowman.' He pointed to the window. 'The hotel has a tiny courtyard that the restaurant looks out on, with a tree and some bushes in it. We could build a snowman.' He grinned at her. 'Let's live dangerously. What do you say?'

'We couldn't.' She shook her head. 'Everyone's asleep. It's probably locked. They wouldn't allow us to do that.'

'There'll be someone on Reception.' He pulled her to her feet. 'I fancy being out in the fresh air for a while.'

So did she. Months of being shut in the antiseptic confines of the hospital had been stifling. 'They'll think we're mad.'

'They're entitled to their opinion.' He bent his head and kissed her once, hard. 'Get dressed in warm clothes. Unless...' he paused as something occurred to him '...you're too tired?'

He meant unless her legs were paining her, Melody thought. And they were, a little, but not half so much as they had in the hospital, when she'd had nothing to think about but how she felt. A feeling of recklessness took hold. 'No, I'm not tired.'

'Come on then. We'll build our very own Frosty for posterity.'

'I hate to remind you, but it'll melt within days.'

'Ah, but the memory won't,' he said, as they left the sitting room for their respective bedrooms. 'And I for one happen to believe that all snowmen come alive the moment they're alone. He'll make the most of his short sojourn here.'

'You're crazy,' she said, laughing. This was all very un-Zeke-like. 'Absolutely crazy. Do you know that?'

'No, just grateful.' His voice was suddenly serious. 'A few months back they were telling me to prepare myself for the worst on that first night they got you into hospital. That kind of experience has a way of making you sort out what's important in life and what's not. You think everything is under control, that you have the future mapped out in nice neat compartments, and then you realise it can change in a moment of time. We're so fragile, us human beings. We break easily.'

'Especially in an altercation with a lorry,' Melody put in dryly, not wanting to continue along that route. 'There is something to be said for the olden days, when it was just horses and carts and Shanks's pony. A wheel over your foot wouldn't have been so bad.'

'I guess.' He smiled, the glint of laugher back in his eyes. 'Although I got kicked by a horse as a child and it's less than pleasant. I was black and blue for weeks.'

There were so many things she didn't know about him. Why it was suddenly so important that she hadn't known about the boyhood incident Melody didn't know, but it was. She turned, opening her bedroom door, and once inside the room dressed quickly in several layers.

The hotel staff would think they'd taken leave of their senses, she thought, as she finally pulled on her thick coat and a woolly hat and scarf. But this beat the many nights in hospital when she'd watched each long hour creep by while the rest of the world slept. Everything was so black in the early hours when you were wide awake and hurting, so hopeless and daunting.

Perhaps she had thought too much? She nodded mentally to the notion. But how could you turn your mind off when sleep wouldn't come? She had refused sleeping pills; she had been on enough medication in the initial days following the accident to last her a lifetime. So drugged up she remembered nothing.

So stop thinking now. Again she nodded mentally. What had that little Irish nurse with the bubbly personality used to say to her? Oh, yes. 'Go with the flow.' And if the flow tonight was behaving like a pair of kids, so be it.

Zeke was waiting for her when she left her room, and once in the lift he dropped a feather-light kiss on her nose. 'You look about ten years old in that hat.' He flicked the bobbles with one finger. 'All bright-eyed and bushy-tailed.'

She smiled. Zeke just looked drop-dead gorgeous.

'And is that good or bad?' she asked lightly, openly fishing for compliments.

'Oh, good—definitely good. I was half expecting you to change your mind about the snowman, to be honest.' He smiled. 'You're always such a stickler for not rocking the boat and playing safe. I didn't think you'd dare face the hotel staff.'

Was she? She stared at him. Probably. Another ghost from her childhood she'd brought with her into adulthood. Her grandmother had definitely been of the old brigade who believed children should be seen and not heard. Part of what had attracted her to Zeke in the beginning was his absolute refusal to accept boundaries, both from outside and within. 'Life isn't a bowl of cherries in spite of what the old song said,' he had told her once. 'It's what you make it, and to win you have to take life by the throat sometimes and force it into submission. Rolling over and playing dead gets you nowhere.'

She hadn't known if she agreed with him at the time, but tonight she knew she did. Keeping her voice light, she said, 'It's not exactly on a par with climbing Mount Everest or journeying down the Amazon, is it? Building a snowman!'

'It's all relative,' he declared firmly. 'One man— or woman's—snowman is another person's Mount Everest.'

The lift doors opened into Reception and he took her hand as they walked across to the desk where the night staff, a porter and a receptionist, were sitting. They looked up in surprise. 'Can I help you, sir?' the receptionist asked politely, professional to the core.

Zeke smiled sweetly. 'We want to build a snowman,' he said blandly. 'In your courtyard. I trust that's okay?'

The receptionist blinked, but recovered almost immediately. She knew who Zeke James was, and it had caused quite a buzz that he was staying at their hotel with his poor wife who had nearly died in that awful accident three months ago. The manager had made it quite clear that whatever Mr and Mrs James wanted, they got. 'Certainly, sir,' she purred smoothly. 'Michael will unlock the door to the courtyard for you. Is there anything you need to—' her pause was infinitesimal '—build your snowman?'

Zeke considered for a moment. 'A hat and scarf would be great. And perhaps a carrot and something for his eyes? You know the sort of thing. Oh, and something that'd do for buttons.'

The receptionist nodded efficiently, and Melody had to bite her lip to stop herself laughing. This was going to be such a good story for the girl among the other staff. The eccentric millionaire to the hilt. She could bring this one out at dinner parties for years to come.

When the said Michael escorted them into the courtyard, which was three or four inches deep in snow, it had stopped snowing. The night was bitterly cold, but crisp and exhilarating, and although the odd window or two which overlooked the courtyard in the hotel glowed dimly, most of them were in darkness. 'I'll go and sort out those items you wanted, sir,' the porter said, obviously tickled pink by the proceedings. 'Lost property should provide the hat and scarf. In these days of political correctness I'd better ask—is the intended snowman male or female? I wouldn't like to presume the gender.'

Zeke smiled. 'I think we'll build one of each. How's that?'

'Right you are, sir. Very wise, if I may say so.'

As the man bustled away, Melody caught Zeke's eye. 'They think we're oddballs. You know that, don't you?'

His smile widened, his voice serene. 'I prefer idiosyncratic myself—and why shouldn't we make the most of it? We've had plenty of winters where it's been damp and wet and miserable in this country. This is—' he paused, staring up into the dark sky above them and then at the white crystallized tree the courtyard contained, made beautiful by its blanket of glistening snow '—special. A night in a million, don't you think?'

He was right. It was. The whole night was special. Special and poignant and unbearably precious. Melody pulled her gloves farther over her wrists. 'Let's get building,' she suggested matter-of-factly, praying he hadn't noticed the tears pricking at the back of her eyes. 'Our offspring are waiting to be born.'

She wished she hadn't said that as soon as the words were out of her mouth. It suggested a permanence which could never be now. But he didn't appear to notice, and soon they were busy with the job in hand. It was hard work, but fun, and she didn't think she had laughed so much for years. The porter returned with the things they'd asked for and then stayed to help for a while. They learnt he had a wife and eight children and twenty-four grandchildren, which was a little staggering, and that every Christmas they all descended for Christmas Day lunch and tea.

'It's mayhem,' he said cheerfully. 'Absolute mayhem. But the missus is only truly happy when the brood's around. Some women are like that, aren't they? Natural mothers.'

Melody smiled and nodded, but his words had struck a chord in her which had been bothering her for a while. Before the accident she had always assumed that eventually she and Zeke would have children, but she had been content to put it to the back of her mind. The act of bringing a child into the world was a huge responsibility, she'd told herself in the rare moments when she'd dwelt on the possibility, and both parents had to be ready for it otherwise it could cause havoc between a couple.

Like it had between her mother and father. Her father had left without even seeing his child, abandoning her mother because he couldn't or wouldn't grow up enough to be a father and husband. And she knew her grandfather had blamed her grandmother for being too tied up with their daughter and neglecting him. Her grandmother had told her that herself. *And so, deep in the hidden part of her, she had reconciled herself to not having children. That was the truth of it.*

She stopped what she was doing and stared at Zeke. And now the very thing she'd decided against was a torment of what she had lost. She wanted his babies. She wanted to have a part of him. Why hadn't she realised it before it was too late? Why hadn't she faced some of those issues and brought them to light? And how could she have been so mixed up for so long without knowing it? Surely other people weren't like her?

'What?' Zeke had been busy rolling a head for the first snowman but now he straightened, his breath a white mist in the freezing air. 'What is it? What's the matter?'

Melody came out of the maelstrom of her thoughts, forcing a smile. 'Nothing,' she said lightly. 'I was just wondering what those little girls we met earlier will say when they see our snow couple in the morning. Perhaps we should build two little ones too. They'd like that. A snow family, like them.'

His eyes narrowed in the way they did when he knew she was prevaricating, but with someone else present he didn't press the issue, and soon they were engrossed in building again. The porter left to find them hot drinks after half an hour, and the two of them worked on in the crystal-clean air.

It took two hours, and several cups of hot chocolate provided by the amenable Michael, but eventually the snow family were finished.

The receptionist came to take a look, smiling at the four figures. 'They're kind of cute,' she said, stifling a yawn. 'Especially the children. Shame they won't last for ever.'

Zeke grinned. 'Thanks for providing the necessary extras.' He turned to Michael, who had joined her. 'I hope we haven't kept you from more important things.'

The porter smiled back. 'What could be more important than a family at Christmas? Even if it is a snow one!' he said quietly. 'Happy Christmas to you, sir. Madam.'

The two hotel staff went back into the warmth, leaving them to survey their handiwork for a moment or two. 'That was quite profound,' Zeke said lazily. 'I think Michael has hidden depths.' He took her arm. 'Come on, let's get you back inside.'

Although her face was rosy with the cold, Melody didn't feel chilled in herself, and she found she didn't want the magical interlude to end. It was Christmas Day, and later in the morning she would walk out of Zeke's life for ever. The break would have to be final, clean and sharp. There could be no meeting up for civilised lunches or dinners, none of the 'we're still good friends' scenarios people they knew indulged in. The past hours had shown her that.

Zeke was irresistible. To her, anyway. To be with him was to want him in every way possible, and so the only option was to remove temptation once and for all. It was quite simple, really.

As they stepped into the heated confines of the hotel from the bitterly cold air outside she shivered convulsively, but the sudden chill was in the essence of her rather than the change in temperature. The night would soon be over.

'You've got cold.' Zeke's voice was concerned. 'We stayed out too long. I wasn't thinking. I'll run you a bath when we get back to the suite. You need to get warm.'

'No, it's fine.' How did you tell the man you loved with all your heart you were leaving? Perhaps you didn't. Maybe the best thing to do was to disappear when the opportunity presented itself? It would avoid the trauma of a final goodbye.

Coward. The accusation was loud in her head and she couldn't argue with it. She was a coward. If she wasn't, she would take the gamble of staying around and seeing what happened.

They reached the lift, and as the doors were closing Zeke curved his arms round her waist. 'We're both cold,' he murmured huskily. 'How about a shower for two, like the old days?'

Her heart stopped and then raced, but through the panic something was clear. She couldn't hide any more. This had always had to happen for him to accept what she had been trying to tell him. He had to see her as she was now—scars and all. She'd had a romantic, idealised idea of leaving him with the image of how she had been—but, Zeke being Zeke, he was never going to let her go if she didn't bare all. Literally. This was necessary, essential. *But, oh, please, don't let me see his face when he looks at me,* she added silently. She wouldn't be able to stand it.

She bent her head, her forehead resting on his wet jacket. 'Your room or mine?' she whispered, keeping her voice steady.

'You choose,' he said softly, hugging her tight.

'Yours.' That way she could leave and find sanctuary in her own room when she needed to. An escape route.

He lifted her chin, kissing her long and hard on the mouth. They were still kissing when the lift doors opened, and he kept his arm round her as they walked into the sitting room of their suite. 'Let's get these wet clothes off you,' he said softly, helping her shrug off her thick jacket and taking her hat, scarf and soaking gloves before pulling off his own. Then he took her cold hand, leading her out of the sitting room and into the corridor towards his bedroom without speaking.

Once inside he went into the bathroom and turned on the water in the shower cubicle. When he returned to the bedroom Melody was standing exactly where he had left her, limbs frozen in fear and embarrassment at the thought of undressing.

'Now to get you all warm and snug again.' He pulled off his jeans, T-shirt and jumper as he spoke, discarding his socks and pants and standing stark naked before her with a supreme disregard of his nudity. He had always been very comfortable with his own body, which didn't make this any easier.

Whether he sensed how she was feeling, Melody wasn't sure, but he didn't attempt to undress her as she had been expecting. Instead he turned and went back into the bathroom, calling over his shoulder, 'Come and join me when you're ready. I'll make sure the water's not too hot.'

She remained perfectly still for a moment, and then

feverishly began to disrobe before she lost her nerve. The bedroom was dimly lit by the same bedside lamp as before, but the bathroom light was stronger, more unforgiving. Once she had shed her clothes she forced herself to move the few steps to the bathroom, her legs wooden. *Get it over with,* she told herself. *Just do it.*

Zeke was in the shower with his back to her, and the air was already steamy because he'd left the door ajar. She stepped into the shower and he turned immediately, wrapping his arms around her. He was already warm and her skin felt icy cold in comparison.

'Just get acclimatised for a minute,' he said huskily, his hands massaging her slender back and shoulder-blades. 'You'll soon warm up, I promise. You're frozen right through.'

Locked together as they were, Melody felt she'd had a moment's reprieve. The spray poured down mostly on Zeke, and after a minute or two he turned her round so the water hit the back of her head in a tingling flood. His hand reached for the shower gel and he poured a little into his palms, lathering it before running his hands over her shoulders and down her arms in firm gentle movements. 'Nice?' he whispered throatily in her ear.

Her nerves were pulled as tight as piano wire, and for the life of her she couldn't reply. He turned her again, his long fingers stroking the white foam across her breasts in slow, sweet languid caresses meant to arouse her, and—in spite of her thudding heart—she felt her nipples tighten under his light touch. Feeling her response, he cupped her breasts in his hands, his thumbs drawing circles round the rosy-pink peaks until they were swollen and aching and she had to bite into her lower lip not to moan out loud. He was so, so good at this.

'So delicious,' Zeke murmured huskily, his mouth finding her eyelids, her nose, and then her lips in a scorching kiss. 'Feeling warmer?'

Unable to speak, Melody managed to nod her head, memories crowding in of times in the past when they had showered together—intimate, precious times. Times of loving and laughter.

With his eyes holding her wide green ones, Zeke lathered his hands again, running them slowly across her belly and then over the rounded swell of her bottom as he moved her sensuously against his hardness. She knew he must have felt the scars at the bass of her spine, but he didn't pause before sliding his fingers over her skin to find the golden curls at the apex of her thighs, his gaze never leaving hers.

Slowly she began to relax, the warm water and his caresses bringing a pleasure that quenched the panic. The worst scars were grooved in the tops of her legs, and standing wrapped together as they were he couldn't see them. For now that was all that mattered. The moment would come, but not just yet.

She reached for the shower gel, her voice soft as she whispered, 'My turn,' longing to run her hands over his body.

'By all means.' His voice was thick with passion and his body demonstrated how much he wanted her, his breathing ragged and his manhood as hard as a rock.

Melody began by soaping the hair-roughened expanse of his muscled chest, flattening her palms over his nipples and rubbing the hard little nubs slowly as she watched his reaction. She took her time, loving the feel of his male flesh, and when her hands slid lower his stomach muscles bunched. Then she found the steely length of his manhood, causing him to gasp as he pulled her closer. 'Hell, Dee,' he muttered thickly.

'I haven't finished,' she protested faintly, wanting him as much as he wanted her and knowing she couldn't wait either.

'Sweetheart, I appreciate the fact you think I'm a control freak, but believe me, I know my limitations,' Zeke said shakily, reaching behind him and turning off the shower. He propelled her out of the cubicle, grabbing two towels off the bath rail and wrapping one round Melody and the other one around his hips.

He pulled her into the darkened bedroom, turning and taking her into his arms as he kissed her hungrily, the towels sliding from their bodies as they fell on the bed. Their bodies were still damp, their hair dripping, but nothing mattered but sating the fierce desire burning between them.

Zeke's hands moved over her feverishly, as though he couldn't get enough of the feel of her, his lips finding the warm pulse in her throat, the rounded swell of her breasts and their swollen peaks, the velvet skin of her belly. When he entered her their bodies moved in a perfect rhythm, building their shared sensation until his final thrust sent them spinning into another world— a world of ecstasy and untold pleasure and splintered light. Melody clung to him, not wanting the moment to end, knowing it would be the last time they'd be like this.

'I love you.' He moved slightly, relieving her of his weight but still keeping his arms round her as he fitted her into his side, pulling the duvet over them.

'I love you.' She could say that and mean it, but her voice was thick with the knowledge that she was going to lose him. 'So much. Always remember that.'

Zeke fell asleep quite quickly, but although she was utterly exhausted Melody couldn't doze off. She lay in his arms, warmly relishing the closeness as her thoughts tortured her. They had made love for a second time and he still hadn't seen what the lorry had done to the once perfect body he had so adored. She had thought the moment had come, and although she had been terrified there had been an element of relief there too. But she'd had yet another reprieve.

She shivered, the slight movement causing Zeke to tighten his embrace in his sleep, but after another moment she carefully extricated herself from his arms and crept out of bed. The hotel room was warm and her hair was almost dry already, but again she felt a shudder run through her.

Quietly she left his bedroom and made her way to her own after picking up her clothes. Once there, she pulled on a pair of leggings and a warm thigh-length top, brushing her hair into submission and then securing it in a high ponytail at the back of her head. Then she walked over to the window and looked out.

It was five o'clock in the morning on Christmas Day. The night hours were almost over. In a little while children all over the country would be waking up to see what Father Christmas had brought them. Houses and flats and apartments would be filled with excitement and noise, and later families would gather together for Christmas lunch. Mothers would be harassed and flushed from working in the kitchen and keeping over-exuberant offspring from raiding their selection boxes, fathers would be playing host and plying visitors with pre-lunch drinks, and grandparents would be arriving with that extra-special present their grandchildren thought Father Christmas had forgotten.

It was a day of busyness and joy and elation, of eating and drinking too much, playing silly games and watching TV. That was normal, the way people did things—only she had never had that experience as a child. Her grandmother had been of the old school. One small stocking hung on the mantelpiece, containing an orange, a monetary gift and a small toy, had been her lot, and Christmas Day had been like any other day except they'd had turkey for lunch followed by Christmas pud. They had spent it alone, and although her grandmother must have received Christmas cards she couldn't remember any. Certainly there had been no decorations nor a tree. After her grandmother had died and she'd been invited to friends' houses for the Christmas break she had been amazed at the furore and excitement, at the sheer pleasure everyone got from the day. It had been a revelation of what Christmas could be.

Why was she thinking of this now? she asked herself, gazing out over the snow-covered buildings beyond the hotel, their rooftops white against the black sky. The past was the past and it didn't do to dwell on it. Her grandmother had done her best and she had always known her grandmother loved her in her own way. She had been fortunate compared to some. Zeke, for instance.

She moved restlessly, suddenly aware of why her thoughts had taken such a turn. Deep inside she had always known Zeke was her chance of experiencing what other people took as ordinary family life. There had been a part of her that had hoped they could create their own world within the world—a place where children could be born and loved and protected, where all the things they'd both missed in their childhood could be given to their babies. She had hoped, but always not quite convinced herself.

And she had never believed she was good enough for him. So she had held back on total commitment, subconsciously waiting for the time when the bubble would burst. She had always been striving towards an unattainable pinnacle of perfection, and although he had taken her as his wife and loved her she hadn't felt she was the best person for him.

Maybe if she had known her mother and father it would have been different—or her mother at least. She had always felt there was so much missing in her background, and her grandmother had been chary about discussing anything. Even the briefest sojourn into the past had brought such bitterness and pain on her grandmother's side she hadn't felt she could press for more. And so she'd grown up wondering, all the time wondering, without any answers about the people who had given her life.

Melody closed her eyes, wrapping her arms round her middle as she shook her head slowly. All this wasn't really relevant to what she was facing now. She was a grown woman of twenty-seven and she had to move on. She had to leave Zeke—go somewhere far away, get a job and carve out some sort of a life for herself. Her thoughts ran through her head, a silent litany. She had told herself the same thing so many times in the past three months, willing herself on.

She couldn't change her mind now. She opened her eyes, beginning to pace the room. She couldn't—didn't dare—let herself imagine anything different, because where would she be then? This way she knew what she was taking on and there was a strange comfort in that, somehow. She'd survive.

She stopped abruptly, feeling as though the walls of the room were pressing in on her. She had always hated small spaces. That had been part of the nightmare of staying in hospital—the feeling of absolute confinement. She needed to get out and walk. It was the only way she could think.

She didn't hesitate. Grabbing a pair of socks from her case, which she still hadn't unpacked, she walked silently into the sitting room and found her coat, hat and scarf, pulling on her boots which were still damp from the snowman exercise. Her gloves she left. They were so sodden she was better off without them.

Slipping the key to the suite in her handbag, she opened the door to the corridor outside and made her way to the lift. When the doors glided open at Reception her heart was thudding. She didn't know what she was going to say to Michael or the receptionist. But as luck would have it Michael was nowhere to be seen and the receptionist was on the phone. She walked quickly across the tiled floor and out of the main doors, giving a sigh of relief when she was in the street.

The cold took her breath away after she had warmed up so nicely, but she walked on. The snow banked either side of the pavement so there was a path in the middle, and she had no trouble reaching the main thoroughfare. She hadn't expected any traffic, it being Christmas Day, but already the city had awoken and yawned life into its inhabitants, and there was the odd person walking here and there, and cars on the roads.

Melody walked with no clear idea of where she was going, taking care to tread carefully. In spite of everything a little frisson of exhilaration curled down her spine. This was the first time she had been out under her own steam—properly out—since the accident, and the independence was heady. It felt good to be part of the human race again.

Although it was still dark, the streetlights combined with the effect of the snow lit up her surroundings perfectly well. She pulled her hat farther down over her ears—it really was bitterly cold—and marched on, wondering why she didn't feel tired. She had felt exhausted yesterday afternoon, and again in the taxi coming back from the theatre, but now she felt as though she could walk for miles.

In spite of coming outside to consider her position with Zeke and what she was going to do, she didn't think as she walked along. She merely breathed in the icy air, luxuriating in the way her face was tingling and the feel of the morning on her skin.

She was alive. She hadn't died under the wheels of that lorry and she wasn't paralysed or confined to a wheelchair. She was lucky. She was so, so lucky. Zeke had been right, and Mr Price too, when they'd said she was better off than lots of the other patients at the hospital.

It was possibly only half an hour later when she realised she needed to sit awhile. Walking in the thick, crunchy snow was more difficult than on clear pavements, and now that the first flush of elation had dwindled exhaustion was paramount. Mr Price had warned her against doing too much initially, she thought ruefully. It would seem he knew her better than she knew herself—which wasn't difficult.

Hyde Park stretched out to the left of her, the trees a vision of Christmas beauty with their mantle of glittering white, but, deciding it was sensible to stay on the main road, she resisted the impulse to wander in.

Instead she brushed the snow off a bench on the pavement overlooking the park and sat down.

A young couple meandered by, wrapped in each other's arms, the girl's ponytail tied with bright red tinsel, a thick strand of which was looped round her boyfriend's neck like a scarf. They smiled at Melody, the girl calling, 'Happy Christmas!' before they ambled on, giggling as they stumbled in the snow.

They probably hadn't gone home yet from some Christmas Eve party or other they'd attended, Melody thought, watching the pair walk on. She suddenly felt aeons old, their carefree faces emphasising her staidness.

She'd never really gone to parties—not until she had met Zeke, that was. Her grandmother hadn't approved of what she'd classified 'aimless frivolity', and even at dance school and in the years following she had preferred to spend any free time practising her dance moves rather than anything else.

No, that wasn't exactly true. Melody frowned as the thought hit. She had always felt guilty if she considered going to parties or get-togethers, knowing the sacrifices her grandmother had undoubtedly made to provide the money for her to follow her chosen career. Add that to the fact that she'd invariably felt like a fish out of water, and had tried to hide herself away in a corner on the rare occasion she'd been persuaded to accompany one of her friends to a shindig, it was no wonder she hadn't been asked much. She'd never felt quite able to let her hair down.

And then Zeke had swept into her life, turning it upside down and challenging all the rules she'd lived by. Her heart thudded, panic uppermost, but she wasn't sure if it was the thought of walking away from him that caused the churning or the fact of how stupid she had been in not making the most of these past few hours when she could still touch and caress him. Why was she sitting on a bench in the middle of a London street when she could be in his arms? Time was so short.

Her toes clenched in her boots but she remained sitting where she was and gradually the panic subsided. She was here because she needed to think. She had been thinking non-stop since the accident, but not coolly or unemotionally. Anything but. She had been jolted to her core and every single thing in her life had been shaken.

It might have been better if she'd been allowed to cry, to sob and howl the frustration and pain at what the accident had taken away from her out of her system, but she had learnt early on that crying unsettled and disturbed the nursing staff. She supposed it had disempowered them in some way, made them feel they weren't doing their job, and because they had all been wonderful to her she'd repressed her grief and got on with the process of building her body. It had satisfied them at least.

A gust of wind feathered the snow on a tree inside the park, missing the ones on either side. She stared at the cascade of white as the cold chilled her skin.

How many times had she asked herself, why her? Why had she had this happen to her? Why had the one thing in her life she was any good at been taken from her? But it was useless thinking like that—as useless as that tree complaining to the wind. *And it wasn't even true.* She was beginning to see that.

Melody was getting cold, but she still sat, her thoughts buzzing. Dancing had been her whole life from as long as she could remember, but that didn't mean she wouldn't be good at something else if she tried. She just never had. Although she might not be able to dance any more, she could teach. At the back of her mind she had always imagined herself doing that one day, just not so soon. She'd thought she would ease herself into it, not have it presented as a *fait accompli*. But why fight it? The accident had happened. End of story.

And Zeke? Could Zeke possibly fit into this new life?

It was as though a separate part of herself was speaking, forcing her to confront the real issue.

It was one thing to decide their marriage was over in the clinical unreal surroundings of the hospital, where life was measured in the regimented hours of an institution, quite another when she was presented by Zeke himself. Dancing had been a vital part of her life, but Zeke—Zeke had been her world. From the first date they'd enjoyed each other's company more than anyone else's, and the intimate side of their relationship had been everything she could have wanted and more. He'd been affectionate and tactile on a day-to-day basis too, often sending her texts out of the blue to say he was thinking of her, and meeting her out of work for lunch or in the evening when she wasn't expecting it.

Her mind grappled with the memories pouring in now she had allowed the floodgates to open. Making love till dawn. Walking on the beach at midnight at the villa in Madeira. Zeke at the stove, cooking breakfast as naked as the day he was born. The list was endless, and after keeping such a tight rein on her mind for the past months she was now powerless to stop the tide. She simply sat, her head spinning and her thoughts bringing a spiralling vortex of emotion that made it difficult to breathe as the sky lightened and dawn began to break.

A new day was dawning, but Melody was anchored to the past, and in spite of her brave thoughts about the future she simply couldn't see a way forward which included Zeke. Their life had been in the spotlight, and because of who he was and the business he'd built up so painstakingly it would continue to be. And something fundamental had changed in her.

Could they function together as a couple, with Zeke living his life and her living a completely different one? Separate not just in their work but in their social life too? She didn't think so. It was a recipe for disaster, however you looked at it.

And so she continued to sit under a pearly white sky, a small figure all alone, huddled up on her bench.

CHAPTER TEN

'Now, I could be wrong, but something tells me you could do with a nice cup of tea, dear. You look frozen to death.'

For a moment Melody couldn't focus on the small plump woman who had sat down beside her on the bench, an equally small and plump dog flopping at his owner's feet. She stared into the rosy face vacantly. 'I'm sorry?' she murmured.

'I walked by this way a little while ago—my Billy still has to have his morning constitutional whether it's Christmas Day or not—and I saw you then. It's a mite cold to be sitting for long, isn't it, dear?' The bright brown eyes were penetrating, but kind. 'You all right? You look all done in.'

Melody tried to pull herself together. Now she had come back to the real world she realised she was absolutely frozen to the core. Her reply of, 'I'm fine, thank you', was somewhat spoilt by the convulsive shiver which accompanied it.

It seemed to have decided her Good Samaritan. The little woman clucked her tongue before saying, 'I always have a cup of tea once I get in, and my place is just across there, dear. Why don't you come in and warm up before you get yourself home?'

'No—no, thank you.' Melody forced a smile as she stood up, only to find she was as stiff as a board. 'You're very kind but I'm perfectly all right. I—I was just sitting awhile.'

'You don't look all right, if you don't mind me saying so.' Obviously plain speaking was the order of the day. 'You're the colour of the snow. Look, my name's Mabel, and I'm not doing anything until my son comes to collect me and Billy later this morning for Christmas lunch at his place. Lovely house he's got—all modern and open-plan, I think you call it. Wouldn't do for me—too much like living in a barn—but it suits him and his wife and the kiddies and that's all that matters. Anyway, I've got an hour or two to kill, and I could do with the company, to tell you the truth. I don't usually mind being on my own—my Billy's good company, bless him—but Christmas Day is different, isn't it? I miss my Arthur then. He died a couple of years ago and I still can't get used to it. Fifty years we were married, and childhood sweethearts. That still happened in my day. Not like now.' This was followed by a loud sniff which eloquently depicted Mabel's opinion of present-day romance.

Melody moistened her lips, ready to refuse the invitation when she caught the fleeting expression in Mabel's eyes. The loneliness connected with something deep inside her, and instead she found herself saying, 'If it wouldn't be any bother I'd love a cup of tea. I didn't realise how cold I'd got.'

'That's right, dear.' Mabel was aglow, standing up and yanking Billy—who had settled himself down for a nap—to his feet. 'Nothing like a cup of tea for sorting things out—that's what I always say. The cup that cheers—that's what my Arthur said.'

Mabel's house turned out to be a well-kept terraced property with an air of faded grandeur and photographs of family adorning every surface in the neat little kitchen-diner Melody was shown into. It was as warm as toast, an Aga having pride of place in the old-fashioned fireplace, and two-cushioned rocking chairs complemented the scrubbed kitchen table and four chairs tucked in one corner. There was a serenity to the house, a quietness that spoke of tranquillity rather than emptiness, which was immensely comforting. Melody had a strange sense of coming home.

'Sit yourself down, lovey.' Mabel pointed to one of the rocking chairs as she spoke. Billy immediately curled up in his basket in front of the range and shut his eyes, as though to say, duties performed; do not disturb.

'Thank you.' Melody sat, somewhat gingerly, and wondered how on earth she had ended up in a total stranger's house on Christmas Day morning, when Zeke was fast asleep in their suite at the hotel. At least she hoped he was asleep. Yes, he would be, she reassured herself quickly. And even if he wasn't it was too late to worry about it. She was here now.

Mabel bustled about making the tea, and when the little woman warmed the teapot and then added two teaspoonfuls of tea from a caddy before pouring hot water into the pot Melody wasn't surprised. Teabags, somehow, weren't Mabel's style.

'Here you are, dear.' Mabel passed her a cup of tea with a thick slice of homemade shortbread in the saucer. 'Now, why, if you don't mind me asking, was a bonny-looking girl like you sitting all by herself on Christmas morning, looking as though she'd lost a pound and found a penny?'

Melody had to smile. No one could accuse Mabel of

beating about the bush. She took a sip of the scalding hot tea and then set the cup in its bone china saucer. 'I don't know what to do,' she said simply. 'Or which way to turn.'

Mabel deposited her dumpy little body in the other rocking chair and smiled placidly. 'A trouble shared is a trouble halved—that's what I always say. So why don't you tell me all about it?' She took a bite of her own shortbread and indicated for Melody to try hers. 'Get yourself on the other side of that, lovey, and tell me what's wrong.'

'It's a long story,' Melody said hesitantly.

'Then all the more reason to get on with it straight away.'

The logic was irrefutable.

An hour and several cups of tea later, Melody was wondering how on earth she could have given her life story to a virtual stranger. Not only that, but she was feeling more relaxed and at home in Mabel's house than she'd felt in years.

Mabel hadn't interrupted her as she'd told her about her childhood, her teenage years, meeting Zeke and all the trauma following the accident. She had simply listened. Billy had twitched in his basket as he'd chased imaginary rabbits, making little growling noises in his sleep now and again as his paws had moved convulsively, but otherwise the kitchen had been quiet and still with no distractions.

'So…' They had sat in silence for a good ten minutes or more, and Melody was half asleep when Mabel broke the peace. 'What are you going to say when you go back to the hotel?'

Melody stared at her new friend. 'I don't know. What

should I do?' Even to herself her voice sounded beseeching.

'I can't tell you, dear, but then you know that. This has to be your decision and yours alone. Only you know how you feel.'

Disappointed, Melody straightened in her chair. 'I can't stay with Zeke,' she said tonelessly, pain tearing through her.

'Can't or won't?' Mabel asked calmly. 'There's a difference. My Arthur and me lost five babies before we had our son. After the fifth, I said I couldn't go through it again. Arthur didn't argue with me, bless him, not even when I decided I couldn't stay here, in this house, with all the memories it held. I wanted to make a fresh start somewhere far away, I told him. Australia, perhaps. I had a brother who'd emigrated and he was doing all right. Or New Zealand, maybe. Anywhere but here, with the little room upstairs decorated as a nursery and the empty cot that had been waiting for a baby for umpteen years.'

Melody was wide awake now, hanging on to Mabel's every word.

'And so I made my plans. Arthur was an engineer, very well qualified and the top of the tree in his own particular field, so we could have gone anywhere and he'd have been sure of work. My brother sent me information on some lovely houses close to where he lived, and a colleague of Arthur's had always said if we ever thought of moving he wanted first option on buying our house, so we didn't even have to worry about selling it. We said our price and he didn't quibble. Arthur gave notice at work, and everything was set for emigrating at the end of May. I remember May twenty-eighth was the day we were going to set sail. Funny how some things stay in your mind, isn't it?'

Melody nodded, transfixed by the drama of the long-ago happenings of the little woman in front of her.

'It was a lovely spring that year—soft and warm and days of endless sunshine all through April. Girls were wearing summer dresses and everyone was happy. Everyone but me. All our plans had gone smoothly, and Arthur had a good job lined up in Australia, but I knew it wasn't right. I wanted to go, I needed to go, but it didn't feel right deep inside—here.' Mabel touched her heart. 'You know? I was running way. I knew it but I wouldn't admit it. And I had good reason for wanting a fresh start—heaven knows I did. I felt I couldn't bear the future if I stayed. The same cycle of hope and then crushing disappointment when my body let me down again.'

Mabel leaned forward, taking one of Melody's hands between her own. 'I felt such a failure, you see. Every time it happened I felt I'd let Arthur down and it was affecting our marriage. I wasn't the girl he'd married, we both knew that, and although he said he loved me just the same, and that as long as he had me it didn't matter if the children didn't come along, I didn't see it that way. I'd even thought about leaving him. He had three brothers and they all had big families, and Arthur was so good with the children—their favourite uncle. I thought if I left him he could have children with some-one else.'

Mabel shook her grey head, making her permed curls bob. 'I was very mixed up. Confused and hurting and trying to be strong.'

'Like me,' Melody whispered, and Mabel squeezed

her hand. 'What happened? Did you get as far as trying out Australia?'

'Arthur's mother came round to see me one morning. It was at the end of April and the sun was shining. I opened the door to her and burst into tears. She stayed the whole day and we talked and talked. I'd lost my own mum years before, and I wasn't one for sharing my troubles with anyone—especially anything private-like. She said something very wise to me that day, and it was a turning point, bless her.'

'What was it?' Melody was holding her breath.

'That the only thing to fear is fear itself. I fought the idea at first, telling myself I wasn't afraid, that it wasn't as simple as that. It's amazing how many reasons you can find to justify yourself when you try. But of course she was right. I was frightened of the future, of trying again, of failing, of losing Arthur's love—a whole host of things. And fear has a way of undermining every foundation in your life, of clouding every issue, especially love and trust. It blinds you.'

'And so you stayed,' Melody said softly. 'You didn't leave.'

Mabel nodded. 'It wasn't a bed of roses, mind. I had to work at it every day. The worries didn't go overnight—they were too deeply ingrained, I suppose—but slowly I saw light at the end of the tunnel, and when I became pregnant again a few months later I believed it would be different and it was. Our Jack was a big strapping baby, with a pair of lungs on him to wake the dead and a smile as wide as London Bridge.'

Melody smiled. 'I'm glad for you, I really am, but your circumstances were different to mine.'

Mabel let go of her hand, but her eyes were tight on the young face in front of her when she said, 'Different circumstances, lovey, but same cause. From what you've told me your Zeke isn't about to change his mind about you because of a few scars. Not now, not ever. And you're running just the same as I tried to do, although I was going farther than you—across the other side of the world. But you could go that far and it'd be the same mistake. Because you can't outrun the fear. You take it with you. When you were talking earlier you called yourself a dancer, but that's not quite right, dear. Dancing was something you did, but it didn't sum up who you are. You're made up of a thousand and one things that make the whole, and by the sound of it that whole is what your husband loves. Same as Arthur loved me.'

Melody gazed into the wrinkled face that was so kind it made her want to cry. 'Zeke said something along those lines,' she admitted quietly, 'but I thought he was just being the dutiful husband and trying to say the right thing to comfort me.'

'There's nothing wrong with that—a bit of husbandly comfort,' Mabel said stoutly. 'But it doesn't mean he didn't mean it. I came to realise that what doesn't break you makes you stronger, as a person and as a couple. That sounds trite, lovey, but I can say it because I've proved it. Young folk today have grown up having everything in life as instant as the coffee they drink, and when something happens that needs a bit of backbone to deal with it half of them are befuddled as to how to cope. You're not like that, and I don't think your Zeke is either.'

Melody thought back over the past twenty-four hours and the hundreds of little ways Zeke had shown he loved her, and wiped a tear from her cheek. 'But he hasn't seen what I look like now,' she whispered. 'And there's so many women out there that throw themselves at him.'

'That's the fear talking again.' Mabel leant forward and patted her hand briskly. 'Now, I'm going to make us another cup of tea and a nice bacon sandwich before you go. Me and Arthur always used to start the day with a cup of tea and a bacon sandwich, but I've got out of the habit since he went. And Melody—' Mabel held her gaze, her voice soft '—don't expect to cross all your bridges in one fell swoop, dear. You'll have good days and bad days, but you'll win through—same as I did. It seems to me that your Zeke needs you every bit as much as you need him. Have you considered that? All those women you talk about were throwing themselves at him for years before he met you, and he didn't fall for any of them, now, did he? Believe in him, lovey. Have faith. Christmas Day is a better day than most to start doing that, don't you think?'

Melody nodded, only half convinced. She suddenly realised she needed to see Zeke again, to look into his face when he said he loved her, into his *soul*. She watched Mabel bustle about the kitchen without really focusing on her. But even that wouldn't be enough. He had to see her as she was now, and it was then she would know. She loved him so much she would be able to read what he felt about having a crippled wife. She would always walk with a limp now, always have a jerky gait, and in the immediate future there were weeks of physiotherapy in store, with possible complications in the way of arthritis and so on as she got older. Their world had been a place of beautiful people—starlets, celebrities, the rich and famous. And botox and plastic surgery when the edges began to fray.

She glanced at her watch and was amazed to see how

the time had gone. It was nine o'clock. Zeke might be awake now, wondering where she was. She had to get back to the hotel.

She gulped down her bacon sandwich, anxious to be gone but not wanting to offend Mabel after all her kindness, and then hugged the little woman before she left the house.

It was bitterly cold outside, but the morning was bright, a high mother-of-pearl sky and a pale sun giving brilliance to the snow-covered world beneath. The city was properly awake now, and although it was not as busy as usual on the main roads, Melody passed lots of pedestrians picking their way along the icy pavements, some with children in tow on new bikes or scooters, which their parents were endeavouring to manipulate through the snow, panting and puffing as they urged their offspring along.

Melody was halfway back to the hotel when she caught sight of Zeke in the distance—a tall, hatless figure head and shoulders above most other folk. Even being so far away she could see his face was as black as thunder. He was angry, furious. Her heart buffeted itself against her ribcage and she stopped, watching him get nearer. He hadn't seen her yet, and she didn't know whether to wave or not. In that first moment of panic if she could have disappeared through the floor out of sight, she would have. He was clearly beside himself.

She had always tried not to upset him in the past. Confrontation of any kind had always crushed her. Not just with Zeke, with anyone, she acknowledged rawly. She had always needed people's approval, or at the very least their acceptance, and to achieve it she had sometimes stifled her own opinions or desires. Somehow the accident had changed that, and she mustn't go back to how she had been. She didn't want to do that. She straightened, her slim shoulders going back as her chin lifted.

Zeke saw her in the next instant, and even from fifty yards away she could see the relief which flooded his taut features. She swallowed, feeling her heart rate skip up another couple of notches, and began walking towards him, wondering how her life had become this constant plunging spiral of emotion. She wanted some kind of normality again. Life would never be humdrum if she stayed with Zeke, she knew that, but their day-to-day existence had been if not ordinary then part of a pattern. The times when they had been alone had not been as many as she would have liked, but there had been the nights locked in his arms when he had been all hers. If only that could happen again.

She didn't know what to expect when Zeke met her. Certainly not the blank face and the voice empty of all expression when he took her arm, saying, 'Let's get back to the hotel.' He suited his long stride to her shorter one, but that was the only concession he made as they negotiated their way along the snowy pavements which were lethal in places.

Melody looked up at him from under her eyelashes, her gaze registering the lines of strain round his mouth and eyes. She had been right. He was angry, but he had been worried too—as she would have been if their positions were reversed. But she'd had to get away for a while, selfish though it had been, although she couldn't expect Zeke would understand that.

'I'm sorry,' she said in a small voice. 'I went for a walk to think. I—I didn't mean to be so long.'

'Some four hours in all, according to the reception-ist who saw you leave the hotel,' Zeke said silkily.

Melody winced. She would have preferred him shouting at her than his dangerously controlled soft tone. It never boded well.

'And it didn't occur to you to ring me and let me know you were all right?' he continued. 'Or even turn your mobile on so I could contact you? But, no, why should it? You're totally in Melody world, aren't you? I'm merely your husband, that's all.'

Melody bit her lip to stop herself firing back. He had every right to be mad. 'I was fine.'

'And I knew that by what? Telepathy? I had no idea where you were when I found you'd gone a couple of hours ago. I've been scouring the streets looking for you and trying to ignore the fact that the river is very deep and very cold.'

'You didn't think—' She stopped, appalled he could imagine she would take her own life. 'You couldn't have imagined…'

'I didn't know what to think, Melody.'

The very fact he had used her full name told her he was beside himself—that and the rigidity of his features.

'I can't reach you, can I? That's the nub of the issue,' he ground out flatly. 'You've shut me out more effectively than I could have imagined. There's no room for me any more. We're not a couple. Perhaps we never were. Maybe all I imagined we had was just wishful thinking on my part.'

She didn't know what to say. That she had hurt him to the core was very clear, but if Zeke held power over her when he was his normal confident, intense and demanding self, it was multiplied a hundred times to devastating effect in his hurt vulnerability. 'I—I thought I could get back before you woke up,' she said weakly, the excuse sounding lame even to her own ears. 'And I didn't mean to be out for so long, but I met someone— an old lady with her dog. We—we talked for a bit.'

'Really? And this old lady and her dog were such riveting company that it completely slipped your mind you had a husband who might—just might—be a tad worried that you had up and disappeared in the middle of the night to goodness knows where?'

'I can't talk to you when you're like this.'

'*You* can't talk to *me*?' He gave a harsh bark of a laugh but didn't slow his footsteps or look at her. 'You're priceless, do you know that? Absolutely priceless. Only you could say that.'

She felt sudden tears burn her eyes, but blinked them away furiously. How ironic that just when she had begun to think they might have a chance he'd decided they were through. He had had enough and she couldn't blame him. She'd acted like a crazy woman over the past months and she couldn't—hand on heart— promise him she was any less scared of the future. He didn't have to put up with this, and why would he?

By the time they reached the hotel her legs were aching badly from the unaccustomed exercise, but she would have walked on hot coals before showing it. They had just entered the lobby when Melody saw the Japanese family, coming from the direction of the dining room, the two little girls clutching beautifully dressed dolls and chattering away to each other. The mother smiled at Melody as they approached, clearly remembering their conversation the day before. 'Santa found his way, as you can see,' she said serenely, secure and content in her role as wife and mother. 'And the reindeers must have enjoyed the carrots because they were all gone this morning.'

'That's good.' Melody stopped and admired the children's toys before saying, 'Have you seen the snow family that came in the night? I think Santa must have brought them too.'

'Oh, yes, they were delighted.' As the father walked on with the children, the mother turned, her voice soft as she said, 'Someone has been very busy.'

The two women exchanged a smile before Melody and Zeke walked towards the lift, and as the doors opened Zeke said flatly, 'How come a stranger gets your smiles?'

Taken aback, she stared at him. 'I'm sorry?'

'It doesn't matter.' He pressed the control panel, and as the lift swept them upwards he thrust his hands deep into the pockets of his trousers, his gaze on his shoes.

'Zeke, please let me explain. Can't we talk at least?'

'Wait.' He raised his head, pinning her to the spot with his ebony eyes. 'Wait till we're in the suite.'

The few seconds until they were standing inside the sitting room seemed like hours, but then Zeke shut the door behind them and Melody forced herself to turn and look at him. His first words took her completely by surprise. 'Is there someone else?'

'What?' She stared at him in utter bewilderment.

'Have you met someone else?' he repeated stiffly.

'Me?' Her voice was a squeak, and she cleared her throat before she managed, 'Of course not. How on earth could I have met someone else when I've been in hospital for the last three months? I've only seen doctors and other patients.'

'Stranger things have happened.'

'Well, not to me.' She struggled to keep her voice steady while anger streaked through her. How could he think that? How *could* he? 'And I resent the question.'

He stared at her intently, and what he read in her face must have reassured him on that point at least because she saw the granite features relax. 'I'm sorry but I had to ask. It would have explained a good few things—not least why you felt it necessary to creep away on Christmas morning and disappear for umpteen hours whilst making sure you were incommunicado.'

'It wasn't like that,' she protested weakly.

'Actually, that was exactly what it was like.'

She watched him take a deep breath and realised he was having difficulty holding on to his self-control. He wanted to yell at her, to shout. He calmed himself with a few more deep breaths and she marvelled at his will-power. 'What I meant was I didn't deliberately not call you,' she said tentatively. 'I simply didn't think.'

'Great. That makes it much better,' he said with grim sarcasm. 'I'm so unimportant I didn't even register on your radar.'

'Stop being like this.' Her voice came out sharper than she had intended—probably because she was desperately trying to keep cool so she could think about what to say, how to reach him. 'I hate it when you're this way.'

His eyes went flint-hard. 'Like what?' he said slowly and deliberately. 'Like I'm angry or hurting or scared rigid? Like I lie awake every night trying to make an impossible situation possible again, knowing I'm up against an adversary who holds all the cards because I love her? My life is falling apart and everything's disintegrating. I am going quietly crazy and I can't concentrate on anything but us. But I mustn't show it. Is that right? Well, tough. I'm human, believe it or not.'

Melody's heart stopped. Zeke was always professional, the consummate business tycoon. No matter what happened he didn't let it interfere with his work. She hadn't really thought about how her accident was affecting him because she had been too caught up in her own pain and grief, but if she *had* given it thought she would have expected he was carrying on as normal, engrossed in the daily exhilarating and hectic whirl that made up his show business empire. But that hadn't been the case at all. And he had already admitted he was blaming himself for not meeting her for lunch that day, as they had originally planned. The guilt of that must have been playing on his mind too. He'd been tormenting himself every bit as much as she had.

She swallowed against the painful lump in her throat as her heart kick-started and then pounded against her ribcage so hard it hurt. How had she missed the fact he was suffering too?

Because she had been so wrapped up in herself, a separate and merciless part of her mind said honestly. So immersed in her battle first to survive and then to claw her way out of the deep fog of despair and depression. And Mabel was right. It was fear which governed her life now. Somewhere in the midst of those first weeks she had let it master her and it had remained in control ever since. It had coloured every thought, every decision.

She had hurt him. Badly. She had pushed him away when he had needed her as much as she had needed him. She had even stopped him visiting her in the hospital. What had he said? That he had resorted to driving to the hospital car park at night just to be near her. Why hadn't she realised he'd been asking for help too? How could she have got it so terribly wrong?

Melody stared at him. He hadn't taken the time to shave when he had found her gone, and his hair looked as though he had run his hand through it a few times—probably in anger. And he had lost some weight over the past months. Altogether he looked harder, sexier and more devastatingly attractive than ever. She loved him, she thought wretchedly. She loved him more than life itself and she had torn them to shreds with her blind stupidity.

She drew in a steadying breath. 'I'm sorry,' she said simply. 'I've done everything wrong and I don't blame you if you're sick and tired of me, if you hate me.'

'Hate you? I love you!' He was shouting now, and it was a relief. 'I love you so much I'm going crazy, woman. What the hell do you want from me, anyway? Tell me, because I'd really like to know. Tell me what to do and I'll do it, damn it.'

Just hours ago she wouldn't have been able to answer him truthfully—especially when he was glaring at her with such deep intensity the black of his eyes glowed like hot coals. 'I want you to keep loving me because I love you and I can't do without you.' There—she had said it, and now the fear was rising up, strangling her, as the enormity of what she'd done washed over her. She stared at him, waiting for his reaction.

Zeke didn't move or even blink for an endless moment, then his whole body relaxed with a deep exhalation. 'Come here,' he said softly, opening his arms. 'We need to talk. I have to understand and you have to open up. But first I need to hold you and convince myself you're really here and not at the bottom of the Thames or in some other guy's arms.'

He held her for a long time without speaking, and although she had wrapped her arms round his waist Melody was aware her heart was pounding like a drum. This was the moment of truth—or at least the next little while would be the moment of truth. Because their talk could only end in one way, and when it did, when they made love, he would look at her scars. They both knew that. The thought made her feel physically sick.

'Okay.' He drew back a little, but only to lead her over to the sofa. 'I'm going to call Room Service before anything else. What do you want to eat and drink?'

'Nothing.' The thought of food was enough to choke her.

Zeke picked up the phone and ordered coffee and croissants for two before coming to sit beside her. 'Tell me where you went this morning first,' he said softly. 'We'll get onto the whys in a minute. I want to know exactly where you've been.'

'I walked for a while, and then sat on a bench and an old lady came and talked to me. She invited me to her house for a cup of tea,' Melody said numbly. 'She—she was kind.'

'Then I'm grateful to her,' he said expressionlessly.

'She told me about her life, how she lost several babies and then went onto have her son. The time... it just went. I didn't realise. I—I think she's lonely in her own way.'

He nodded. 'And do I take it this conversation was a two-way thing? That you told her about our problems?'

She was touched he said 'our', when he could, in all honesty, have said 'yours'. It was her turn to nod.

'This is not a criticism, more of an observation,' Zeke said carefully. 'You could spend four hours talking to this old lady about how you were feeling, but you can't share it with me?'

Melody couldn't let that go unchallenged. 'I didn't spend four hours with her. It was two at the most—

probably only one and a half. And I *have* talked to you about everything.'

'No, Dee, you've talked *at* me, when you have talked at all. You've given me a list of reasons why the thought of staying with me is impossible—none of which I buy, incidentally. In fact you couldn't come up with a reason for us to split because there isn't one. From day one I knew we were going to be together. I told you that often enough. But you never believed me, did you? It never sank in. Even after two years of marriage.'

She stared at him, her eyes huge in her white face. 'I wanted it to be true.' She swallowed painfully. 'I really did.'

'But you never *believed* it,' he said softly. 'No matter what I said or what I did you didn't believe it.'

She couldn't deny it. Some inbuilt survival instinct had prevented it. If she had let herself accept she was the only one for Zeke—his 'dream woman', as he'd often described it—the risk would have been too great. Once she had relied on him to that extent she'd never have recovered if it all went wrong. Her voice was a tiny whisper when she said, 'I suppose I couldn't believe someone like you would want someone like me for ever.'

Zeke's fingers took hold of her face and his dark eyes stared straight into hers. 'What do you mean, someone like you? You're beautiful, exquisite, unique—the best there is. And the amazing thing, the thing I couldn't get my head round at first, is that you're as lovely on the inside as the outside. The first time I met you—when you were late for the audition, you remember?—I wanted you physically. You danced as though every bone in your body was fluid, flowing with the music, and it was the most erotic thing I'd ever seen. And then you stood in the middle of the stage and refused to be intimidated by my questions or by me. A little firebrand, gusty and defiant. And then I heard you talking with the other girls and I found out the reason you were late was because you'd taken pity on an old woman who was devastated by the loss of her cat. Those other girls couldn't understand it. There wasn't one of them who would have done the same. I couldn't understand it. You were an enigma. I had a job to believe you were real.'

'Me?' Fascinated as she was by his description of her, she found it hard to believe he was talking about ordinary, run-of-the-mill Melody James.

'Your soft centre is something I have no defence against, my love,' Zeke murmured huskily. 'It melts me, it ties me up in knots, it makes me want to be a better man than I am and to believe that good can triumph over bad—that Father Christmas really does exist, and that roses round the door and happy-ever-after is there for the taking.' And then he smiled. 'Don't look like that. Don't you know how much I adore you?'

No. No, I had no idea. 'Of course I do.'

'Liar.' It was without heat. 'Sweetheart, you penetrated my heart as easily as a knife through warm butter. I won't pretend there were times when I was frustrated I couldn't do the same with you. But I'm a patient man.'

Zeke? Patient? He had many attributes, but patience wasn't one of them. And he did have her heart. He always had.

Something of what she was thinking must have shown in her face, because he smiled again, his voice soft when he qualified, 'Semi-patient at least—for you, that is.' He bent and pressed a kiss on her mouth, pressed another to the tip of her nose and onto her forehead, before settling back and surveying her with ebony eyes. 'So, tell me why you banned me from visiting you in hospital, and why your solicitor told my solicitor you want a divorce,' he said levelly, no inflection in his voice. 'And why, after we made love—twice—you still felt the need to escape and put some distance between us.'

CHAPTER ELEVEN

THE arrival of the coffee and croissants a moment or two after Zeke had demanded she talk to him delayed the inevitable by a few minutes. Melody didn't want to eat or drink, but she did both to gain a few precious get-your-facts-straight moments. The coffee was too strong, and the croissant she forced down didn't sit well with Mabel's bacon sandwich, and when she had finished Zeke's eyes were still waiting for her to begin.

Her heart was thumping in her chest, staccato-beating in her ears, because she knew she had to get this right. She had to make him understand why everything she had done since the accident was wrong. All her past had come together when she'd woken up in that hospital bed, and from that moment she had been in a vacuum of fear and confusion, sucked into a dark and terrifying merry-go-round of hopelessness.

She cleared her throat. 'I haven't been thinking clearly over the last weeks.' To give him his due, he didn't raise his eyebrows in the quirky, sarky way he did sometimes. Neither did he make any of the hundred and one responses he could have made in the circumstances. He simply sat looking at her. She didn't know if that made it easier or harder.

'I've realised this—my freaking out in the hospital and asking you for a divorce and everything—is because...' She paused and swallowed hard. 'I was frightened you wouldn't want me any more now I'm— I'm disfigured.' She rushed on quickly before he could speak. 'Not that you have ever done or said anything to make me think that way. I know it's me. Mabel—the lady I met today—said I was letting fear rule me, and she's right. It's just that I know you appreciate grace and beauty more than most. Partly due to your—your beginnings and everything, and there's nothing wrong with that. But—but I'll never dance again. I'm...different now.'

'Sweetheart, your legs were messed up. I know that's one hell of a big deal for you, because dancing is your life, but I can help you through it. This doesn't have to be the end of using the fantastic gift you've been given, just rechannelling it. I've got a couple of ideas about that, but they can wait. The main thing I have to convince you of right now is that your grace and beauty has never depended on your dancing. You are grace and beauty. Those qualities are in every word you speak, the way you are, every look and movement you make. The lorry couldn't take them away from you, don't you see? You're my sweet, generous, incomparable baby— my darling, my love.'

She was falling apart, her eyes blinded by her tears, and when he took her in his arms again she fell against him, needing his strength and security as never before as she sobbed against his broad chest.

'What?' He bent his head to her, her incoherent words punctuated by convulsive shudders. 'What did you say?'

'I—I—' Melody made a huge effort and sat up, taking the handkerchief he gave her. 'I don't see how you can think of me in that way. It's like you're talking about someone else.'

'Then you'll just have to take it on trust until I can convince you,' he said softly. 'And if it takes a lifetime I'll do it. You're mine, Dee, every bit as much as I am yours. You are the only person I could have possibly ended up with, and if we hadn't met—if we'd missed each other somehow—I'd have gone on as I was. Happy in a way, fairly okay with myself, but with a huge reservoir inside me which would have remained untapped. I've heard it said that there are several people in the world that someone can love if they meet them, but it's not that way with me. You saved me. That's the only way I can put it.'

He had never told her this before—not in so many words—and yet now when she thought about it she realised his whole way with her had demonstrated it from the beginning. She smiled tremulously and blew her nose, shaking back her hair from her damp face, and then lifted one trembling hand to his face. 'I love you,' she said very quietly. 'I always have and I always will. There will never be anyone but you for me.'

He smiled a singularly sweet smile as his hand covered hers. 'Then there's nothing we can't overcome.'

She nodded, relaxing into his embrace as he reached for her but knowing deep inside that she was still frightened by what lay ahead. She hated that she felt that way, but she couldn't help it.

He tilted her face to meet his, covering her lips in a fierce kiss of such hunger that she immediately responded to the deep, unspoken need. His mouth was still hard on hers as he stood and picked her up in his arms, carrying her into his bedroom as he crushed her against him. Lying her on the bed, he bent and stretched out beside her, but he didn't immediately begin to undress her or himself, wrapping his arms round her in a gesture intended to comfort as he kissed her again.

The kiss deepened, becoming one of such explosive warmth that sexual feeling flowed through her as hot and smooth as melted honey, and she sighed in pleasure, curving into him as though she would fuse their bodies together. He pulled his mouth away for a millisecond to fill his lungs, and then the sensual onslaught began anew as he tangled one large hand in her hair, continuing the magic of his kisses as his lips travelled over her cheeks, her closed eyelids, the arch of her fine brows before returning to reclaim her mouth once more.

He kissed her for a long time as his hands roamed over her body on top of her clothes, cupping her breasts and shaping the plump mounds with his palms as his thumbs teased her nipples into hard peaks. Winter sunlight spilled onto the bed from the large window, splintered yellow against her closed eyelids which enclosed her in a world of pure sensation.

She was aware of him divesting himself of his clothes, although his mouth barely left hers, and then he expertly removed her top and her lacy bra. His mouth moved from hers, lingering for a moment over her collarbone as his lips stroked the silky skin, and then he reached the soft fullness of her aching breasts.

Melody moaned throatily as his mouth fastened on one erect nipple and he gave it loving attention before moving onto its twin. 'Exquisite,' he murmured softly. 'Such wonderfully large rosy nipples. You taste of molasses and roses, do you know that? Sweet and scented and deliciously ripe. I want to devour you. I can't get enough of you.'

He continued to please her with lips and tongue until

she dug her fingers into his muscled shoulders, murmuring something incoherent even to herself. It seemed impossible so much feeling, such emotion, could be contained in her body without her splintering into a million pieces.

'I want to kiss every inch of you,' he whispered, his mouth returning to her lips for a moment. From being fluid she stiffened as she felt him peeling off her leggings and lace panties, but almost immediately he was lying against her again, holding her close so her breasts came into tender contact with his chest. The friction of his body hair against her engorged breasts was tantalising, but reality had caused her to become tense in his arms and she didn't know how to pretend. She didn't actively resist him, but the thudding of her heart now had nothing to do with sexual desire and all to do with panic.

He kissed her once more before he said, very softly, 'Dee? Look at me. Open your eyes. Look at me, sweetheart.'

She couldn't. Ridiculous, but she couldn't. She was too terrified of what she might read in his face. Kindness and pity would be worse than distaste.

'Please, sweetheart.' He stroked a strand of silky hair from her brow. 'Look at me.'

Slowly she forced her eyes open. He was smiling. Funny, in all her nightmares she hadn't considered that, but she might have known Zeke would surprise her.

'The worst is over,' he said, sheer love shining from his eyes. 'You've faced your fear and now we move on. You won't believe you're more beautiful and desirable to me than ever for a while. I understand that. But your scars aren't ugly to me, darling. They remind me I'm the luckiest man in the world, because I came close to losing you and I was spared the unthinkable. I couldn't have gone on without you. I know that.'

Her eyes traced the contours of his face, taking in the velvet black eyes, the sloping lines that created his firm mouth, the straight solid shape of his nose. She searched each feature, looking for the barest hint of disgust but there was none. He was just her Zeke, her babe. She had always called him that, babe, although she didn't know why. She had certainly never felt inclined to do the same with anyone else.

Her hands had been knotted against his chest, but now they slowly uncurled as he kissed her again, his tongue rippling along her teeth until she opened to him. He wrapped the long swathe of her strawberry-blond hair around his fingers, tilting her head back slightly as he ravaged her mouth. Each movement he made exploded more desire in her veins, radiating throughout her body with a drowsy warmth that was voluptuous and sensual. She had missed him. She had missed him so much, the longing for his presence and body so intense she'd had to shut it out of her consciousness or go mad with the need. But now there was no need to fight the passion and love and desire. She could give in to those deepest inner needs.

She closed her eyes, curving into his hard male frame and sighing with sheer ecstasy as she drifted off into a place of bliss.

CHAPTER TWELVE

MELODY stretched slightly, drowsily aware she was enclosed in a cosy cocoon. She cuddled deeper into the animal warmth that was the source of her satisfaction, her limbs heavy and relaxed. Quite when she became aware of the fact that a hard muscular forearm was curved over the dip in her waist she wasn't sure. It could have been minutes or hours. But suddenly she was wide awake, her eyes opening.

'Hi.' Zeke's voice was lazy and his kiss was deep and slow.

Her green eyes stared into ebony. 'I fell asleep.'

He grinned, apparently not in the least put out. 'That you did,' he agreed smokily. 'Which was a first for me.'

Melody didn't know where to put herself. The culmination of months of anguish, worry and heartache and she had fallen asleep under Zeke's lovemaking. She hadn't meant to. She had been there with him every inch of the way—or so she had thought. 'I'm sorry,' she murmured helplessly. She remembered him kissing her after he'd undressed her, reassuring her, and then... 'I must have been more tired than I thought.'

His grin widened. 'But you've had a nap,' he pointed out softly, enfolding her in a tender yet hungry embrace, his hands stroking down her spine from her shoulders into the concavity of her tiny waist and to the seductive flare of her hips as his tongue drew an arc round the curve of one ear before his teeth gently closed on the lobe. 'And it hasn't been that long. I bet the coffee is still warm in the pot out there.'

They didn't put it to the test. They explored each other with sensual and hungry abandon, loving each other with a need which did away with any thought of shyness or restraint. Zeke's fingers slipped down the length of her, defining her neatly rounded bottom with a languid caress as he pulled her into the hard strength of him. Even when his hands moved over the base of her spine and the tops of her legs she didn't flinch, putting her hands to either side of his face as she pulled him down to meet her in a kiss that was as fierce as it was gentle.

The blood in her veins rushed to nourish the surface of her skin, a rosy glow turning her flesh translucent and releasing her intimate perfume. By the time he levered his body over hers she was aching for him, the feel of his arousal an aphrodisiac in itself. She couldn't contain the desperate little whimper of desire that broke from her lips, needing him deep inside her, wanting the feeling of oneness, of closeness.

With one sure thrust Zeke entered the silken sheath that welcomed him, Melody's muscles tightening to lock him into her. The rhythm of their shared passion mounted, and with each movement Melody felt they were reaffirming those vows they had taken two years ago, but with a special meaning now. Then they had been madly in love, giddy and intoxicated with the thrill of the newness of it all. Now they had come through the fire and their joining was all the more intense and passionate because of it. It was as though their very souls were merging and they were equal in their drawing strength from each other, their entwined bodied fitting together in a manner as old as time and as sweet.

Zeke filled her completely, the sensation extremely satisfying as he built their rapture until she thought she would float right out of her body into somewhere beyond time. When the culmination came its violence sent them both over the edge of reality. In all the times they had come together—times of deep passion and erotic exploration and need—it had never been so cataclysmic, and she knew he felt it too. He held her hard against him, his body trembling with the aftermath of their lovemaking as he kept her intimately joined to him.

'I love you.' His voice was deep and warm and very sensual. 'More than life itself.'

'I love you too,' she whispered shakily.

He searched for something in the depths of her eyes and then kissed the tip of her nose. 'You're addictive, do you know that? Before I collected you from the hospital I promised myself I'd take it nice and easy. I'd just be there for you, no pressure, no strain, taking it as slow as you wanted. And now in the space of a few hours I've made love to you three times. My only excuse is that for the last three months I've lain awake each night in our bed wishing you were there with me, remembering how it was, driving myself crazy.'

He withdrew from her body but his arms came around her, binding her to him in a constrictive circle as he whispered, 'I can't believe you're here now. When I woke up earlier and found you gone...'

She cupped his rugged face with her small hands, kissing him hard. 'I'm sorry,' she said gently. 'I won't do that again. I promise. I'm here now.'

He kissed her back, even harder, stroking her warm flesh as he moved her against him. 'In mind as well as body?' he asked quietly. 'And don't pretend to make me feel good. I need to know how you're feeling if we're going to beat this thing.'

In reply she curved her body around his, delighting in the way they fitted together. 'I'm here,' she repeated firmly. She slid her fingers over the damp skin on his back, powerful muscles responding under her touch before she stroked her way round to his flat belly, teasingly following the line of hair which arrowed downwards before flaring dramatically out again and providing a thick dark cradle for his masculinity. When her hand circled and caressed the erection her touch had brought forth, she smiled at him seductively. 'Fancy making that four times you've forced your wicked way on me?' she murmured throatily, kissing the corner of his mouth tenderly.

This time their loving was long and slow and infinitely satisfying, and when they had come back from the world of intimate light and sensation, Melody lay in her husband's arms, her whole body so relaxed it felt boneless as Zeke pulled the duvet over them. The events of the past twenty-four hours and not least the weeks of misery and anxiousness before Christmas had caught up with her, but she didn't want to sleep again. She just needed to be with Zeke, to feel him, look at him, touch him. She felt as though she had been on a long, dangerous journey and come home. Softly, she murmured, 'You said you had some ideas about what I can do in the future earlier?' She twisted to face him. 'What are they?'

He cupped her buttocks and pulled her tightly against him, his mouth taking hers in a long kiss. When at last he released her lips he still held her close. 'That I have,' he agreed huskily. 'How about I go and fetch us a drink and we'll talk? There's wine in the fridge.'

She grinned at him. 'Isn't it a bit early in the day for wine? It isn't even lunchtime yet.'

'Not at all. It's Christmas Day. Ordinary rules don't apply. Besides, it'll give you an appetite for lunch— which, incidentally, I suggest we have here in bed. In fact I see no reason for us to get up today, do you?'

She gazed at him, loving him and thanking God that Christmas Eve had worked its magic and brought her to her senses. 'None at all,' she said softly.

The wine was icy cold and delicious when he brought the bottle and two glasses back to bed, along with the rest of the presents from under the tree in their little sitting room. She opened her presents in his arms, delighting in the dainty little gold wristwatch, gossamer-thin silk nightdress and negligee, her favourite perfume and other gifts, all perfect and chosen with love. But it was the eternity ring nestled between her engagement and wedding ring her gaze kept returning to. The ring was exquisite, but it was the statement behind it that made it precious beyond words. He had bought it when she had rejected him, spurned his love and refused to listen to him, because he loved her and was determined love was eternal. And it was. Oh, it was.

'Before I make my suggestions about the future, can I just say they are meant to fit in with you having my babies?' Zeke said softly as she snuggled down in his arms again.

Zeke's babies. She could let herself believe it would happen now. She smiled at him, radiant in a way he hadn't seen before and so beautiful she took his breath away. 'That might happen sooner than you think,' she said serenely. 'We've made love four times in the middle of my cycle and I haven't been taking the pill since I've been in hospital, so...'

'You wouldn't mind?' he asked, a touch anxiously.

She touched his face lovingly. 'Would you?'

'I can't wait to have you barefoot and pregnant,' he said with deep satisfaction. 'And it would fit in well with certain changes I've made in my own life in the last little while.' He smiled at her frown of enquiry before kissing her.

He reached for their wine glasses, topping them up and handing her hers before he said, 'A toast to the new owner of Media Enterprises—David Ellington.'

She stared at him in amazement and shock. 'You've sold your business?' David Ellington was a mogul billionaire.

'Lock, stock and barrel,' he said cheerfully, taking a gulp of wine. 'I should have been with you the day of the accident instead of chasing my tail over some damn crisis or other. It was a wake-up call—a terrifying one. I vowed the night of the accident that if you pulled through I'd reassess what was important in my life. So I did. It didn't take much thought.'

Melody was horrified. His empire was hard-won. He had built it up brick by brick and she knew he was immensely proud of what he had achieved. 'You shouldn't have done that,' she whispered. 'Can't you change your mind?'

'Too late.' He smiled at her. 'And it's *exactly* what I should have done. You confirmed that yourself yesterday. You told me you needed to make a new life, separate from the hectic entertainment business we've been involved in, something that would cut out the excess of parties and other functions that took up so much of our time. Independently of you I had come to the same conclusion. It would have happened sooner or later once we'd decided to start a family. The accident merely precipitated things. You were right when you said there were too many people wanting a piece of me, but wrong when you thought you were just one of them. That was never true, however you felt. I didn't feel it was the moment to tell you I'd sold up yesterday—there were other things to sort out first. But when I said to you I could give it all up and walk away without a backward glance or any regret, it was because I had done exactly that. My world was never the business or the contacts I'd made or the power games. Not after I had met you. You are my world, Dee. We've spoken about a family but if the children didn't come along for whatever reason I would still consider myself blessed among men. You're my sun, moon and stars. The centre of my universe.'

He touched her stricken face gently, stroking down her cheek and round her full lips with the tip of his finger. 'I'm glad it's gone, Dee. Truly. It was a stage of my life which was enjoyable while it happened, but I want to move on with you. It's also made us a great deal of money,' he added with male satisfaction. 'More than enough for us to do anything we want for the rest of our lives.'

She could still hardly take it in that he had actually walked away from his empire. But if he had told her instead that he intended to sell she would have thought he didn't mean it, she realised now. Was that why he'd made it a *fait accompli*? She would have felt guilty, felt he was only doing it for her, and would have attempted to persuade him they could go on as they had been.

Maybe he knew her better than she knew herself? On second thought there was no maybe about it.

'Thank you,' she murmured softly.

Suddenly she felt as if a huge weight had been lifted. No more premières and red carpets and first-night parties. No more relentless rounds of functions and shows and receptions where you couldn't wear the same dress twice or the knives would be out—always in the back. Of course some of the social occasions they'd attended had been fun, and overall she had enjoyed herself and relished being on Zeke's arm as his wife, but the accident had changed something independent of the damage to her legs, and she wouldn't have wanted to step onto the merry-go-round again. And now she didn't have to. But at a huge cost to Zeke.

'What will you do?' she asked him tremulously, not knowing if she wanted to laugh or cry. He wasn't the kind of man who could sit and do nothing.

'Again, let me qualify,' he said, settling her more comfortably in the circle of his arms. 'This all has to fit in with what I see as my main job of being a husband and father, okay?' He waited for her nod before continuing, 'I have a couple of ideas, and they could run alongside the treatment programme your doctors and I have worked out, which will take one day out of the week every week for some time but could result in practically full mobility after six months or so, and excellent long-term prospects. There's a Swiss doctor I've got on board who specialises in your sort of injuries— there's no one to beat him, not even in the States—and he's confident you'll be walking normally by this time next year.'

She half lifted herself on one elbow and kissed him with single-minded intensity and sweetness. Just knowing he was ready to stand and fight with her was everything, and whether she regained all she'd lost didn't matter so much now.

Zeke lifted strands of her hair and twined them round his fingers as he kissed her back just as strongly, and then he dropped a kiss on the end of her nose as he drew back a little. 'First idea,' he said matter-of-factly. 'We look for suitable premises and open a drama school for under-privileged youngsters. It would be the real McCoy, for kids from nine or ten upwards, so we'd need to employ teachers for the normal subjects as well as those specialising in drama and dance and so on. It could be a boarding school for those who wanted it, and a home 365 days of the year for others who need it. Children who have been kicked from pillar to post, kids in the care system or in dysfunctional homes. They'd all have to have a leaning towards acting or singing or dancing, but once they were with us they'd be there until they chose to leave. And the home part of the place would be exactly that—not an institution. A place of security and unconditional support.'

The sort of place he would have longed for as a confused and troubled boy, Melody thought, her understanding causing her to swallow the lump in her throat. Oh, Zeke, Zeke.

'Of course you'd be in charge of the drama side— the hiring of staff and so on—and I thought you might want to be hands-on teaching dance? We'd need an establishment with plenty of grounds for a swimming pool, tennis court and so on, and a house separate from the school for us would be essential. I've no real idea of the mechanics of it all, but I know people who could make it happen as long as the funding was in place.'

'And we could afford to do that?' she asked softly.

Zeke smiled. 'Several times over, sweetheart.' He guided her glass of wine to her lips and took a sip of his own before he went on, 'There are other options, of course. You might like to travel for a year or two once your treatment is over—a world tour, staying over for as long as you like if a particular place takes your fancy. Or we could run our own theatre? Something in that line? Or you could run a traditional dancing establishment?'

Melody came straight back to the idea that had fired her imagination. 'This drama school—wouldn't it be a huge undertaking to do it properly?'

'Massive,' he agreed. 'The dance side would involve performance, choreography, management and dance theatre, including the history of dance and related arts, aesthetics and critical studies, production, music accompaniment and composition, and that's without the drama side. Acting, directing, technical aspects, backstage crafts and writing for the stage would all be necessary, along with practical theatre.'

He paused for breath and Melody stared at him in wonder. 'You've really looked into this, haven't you?'

Zeke nodded. 'It would be a total life change, Dee. But one which would fit with family life if it was done properly. We would afford to get the best folk for the children on board, people of like mind, and I thought—' He stopped abruptly and she saw a muscle clench in his square jaw.

'You thought?' she pressed quietly.

'We could make a difference. Not to every child, perhaps—I am a realist—but for the ones we give direction and purpose to it would be worth it. But it's only an idea.'

She buried her face in his neck for a moment, overwhelmed at the turn their lives had taken. This was perfect, so utterly perfect. And only Zeke could have thought of it.

'Dee?' His voice carried a note of anxiety. 'You don't have to say anything until you've thought about it. It's a big deal—'

She stopped him by winding her arms around his middle as she lifted her face to his. 'I love you, I love you,' she said, over and over again so he would know. 'And I can't think of anything better. Think of it, Zeke. Children who have nothing, given a foundation and a pride in the gift they have. Do you really think we can do it? Provide them with a home and hope?'

'Of course.' The words were pronounced emphatically, a declaration, and she knew in that moment he would make it happen.

She reached up and placed her mouth on his. It wasn't often she made the first move, and his reaction was immediate and fierce as he crushed her into him, kissing her with a hunger that touched her to the core. He kissed her for a long time as they murmured incoherent words of love, drawing strength from each other. 'I can do anything with you by my side, but without you I'm nothing,' he muttered desperately. 'Never leave me like you did this morning—without a word, a goodbye. I thought I'd lost you. I need you, sweetheart. You've got no idea how much.'

'I think I have, because I need you every bit as much,' she whispered brokenly. 'I've been so miserable. Not because of the accident and knowing I'd never dance again, but because I thought I had to let you go. You're my world, my existence.'

He gave a choked laugh. 'So we've both been tearing ourselves apart because we love each other?'

She smiled tremulously. 'Maybe we aren't the smartest kids on the block,' she admitted weakly. Joy, like warm honey, was spreading through her body with healing reassurance. She could believe this. She could trust him. She had wasted weeks of her life letting fear dictate her actions and rule her mind, but no more. She must have been crazy—stark, staring mad—to imagine Zeke would look at another woman or walk away from her. He wasn't like her father or her grandfather. He was unique and all hers. Her husband, her love, her life.

They held each other tightly until the crescendo of emotion descended to a more controllable plane, and after one more long, lingering kiss she snuggled into him with her head on his chest. 'I booked in to this hotel for a few days,' she whispered drowsily, after a minute or two of listening to the steady beat-beat of his heart beneath her cheek. 'We can spend them all in bed, can't we? Have all our meals here?'

She knew he was smiling. She could read it in his voice when he murmured, 'Sure thing,' as his hands wandered soothingly over her skin, stroking her neck, her shoulder, her back in light caresses. 'We've got some time to make up and I can't think of a better place to do it. Besides, plenty of sleep, plenty of exercise—of the most beneficial kind,' he added, squeezing one rounded buttock to give emphasis to his words, 'along with good food and drink is just what you need. This is our time. No one knows where we are, the phone won't ring, and my mobile's switched off. There'll be no taps at the door apart from Room Service.'

'Mmm.' Heaven on earth. Melody closed her eyes and felt herself gradually drift towards sleep. Zeke's breathing had become slow and steady and she knew he'd fallen asleep, but one arm was draped over the dip in her waist and the other hand was tangled in her hair as though even while he slept he needed to know she was secure and within his grasp.

She thought of the snow family in the courtyard and smiled dreamily. Last night had been magical and infinitely precious, but they had the rest of their lives to look forward to now. Nights locked in each other's arms and days spent together as they worked to bring hope to children who expected none, who were damaged like Zeke had been. This was a new chapter, a new beginning, and when the babies came—Zeke's babies—they would be loved as neither of them had been loved when they were young. Their children would grow up strong and secure in their parents' love—she and Zeke would make sure of that—each one knowing they were precious and unique.

Zeke stirred slightly, drawing her even closer as he murmured her name in his sleep, and as she floated into a warm, soft, safe place she knew that to him she was everything—the only woman he could ever love, complete and whole. And because he thought she was beautiful she was.

Sleep crept up on her, and in her hazy contentment she thought of Mabel and her wise words. She would go and see the old lady again, and take Zeke with her this time. She felt they were meant to be good friends, and the loneliness she had sensed in the brave old soul could be channelled to some extent. Children loved a grandmother figure, and always responded to dogs too. She could see Mabel joining them for days out once the school was up and running, and she was sure the old lady would play her part in counselling hurting little hearts the same way Mabel had comforted her that morning.

She slept, and the two of them continued to lie wrapped closely in each other's arms—two hearts that beat as one, two minds intrinsically linked for eternity with that most powerful and sweetest of bonds, true love.

They had come through the fiery furnace. They were home.

* * * * *

CLASSIC

Quintessential, modern love stories
that are romance at its finest.

REQUEST YOUR FREE BOOKS!

2 FREE NOVELS PLUS
2 FREE GIFTS!

PASSION GUARANTEED SEDUCTION

*Brittany Grayson survived a horrible ordeal at the hands
of a serial killer known as The Professional…
who's after her now?*

*Harlequin® Romantic Suspense presents a new installment
in Carla Cassidy's reader-favorite miniseries,*
LAWMEN OF BLACK ROCK.

Enjoy a sneak peek of
TOOL BELT DEFENDER.

*Available January 2012
from Harlequin® Romantic Suspense.*

"**B**rittany?" His voice was deep and pleasant and made
her realize she'd been staring at him openmouthed through
the screen door.

"Yes, I'm Brittany and you must be…" Her mind suddenly went blank.

"Alex. Alex Crawford, Chad's friend. You called him
about a deck?"

As she unlocked the screen, she realized she wasn't
quite ready yet to allow a stranger inside, especially a male
stranger.

"Yes, I did. It's nice to meet you, Alex. Let's walk around
back and I'll show you what I have in mind," she said. She
frowned as she realized there was no car in her driveway.
"Did you walk here?" she asked.

His eyes were a warm blue that stood out against his
tanned face and was complemented by his slightly shaggy
dark hair. "I live three doors up." He pointed up the street to
the Walker home that had been on the market for a while.

"How long have you lived there?"

"I moved in about six weeks ago," he replied as they

walked around the side of the house.

That explained why she didn't know the Walkers had moved out and Mr. Hard Body had moved in. Six weeks ago she'd still been living at her brother Benjamin's house trying to heal from the trauma she'd lived through.

As they reached the backyard she motioned toward the broken brick patio just outside the back door. "What I'd like is a wooden deck big enough to hold a barbecue pit and an umbrella table and, of course, lots of people."

He nodded and pulled a tape measure from his tool belt. "An outdoor entertainment area," he said.

"Exactly," she replied and watched as he began to walk the site. The last thing Brittany had wanted to think about over the past eight months of her life was men. But looking at Alex Crawford definitely gave her a slight flutter of pure feminine pleasure.

Will Brittany be able to heal in the arms of Alex, her hotter-than-sin handyman...or will a second psychopath silence her forever? Find out in
TOOL BELT DEFENDER
Available January 2012
from Harlequin® Romantic Suspense
wherever books are sold.

Harlequin® *Desire*

ALWAYS POWERFUL, PASSIONATE AND PROVOCATIVE.

USA TODAY BESTSELLING AUTHOR

KATHIE DeNOSKY

BRINGS YOU ANOTHER STORY FROM

TEXAS CATTLEMAN'S CLUB: THE SHOWDOWN

Childhood rivals Brad Price and Abigail Langley have found themselves once again in competition, this time for President of the Texas Cattleman's Club. But when Brad's plans are interrupted when his baby niece is suddenly placed under his care, he finds himself asking Abigail for help. As Election Day draws near, will Brad still be going after the Presidency or Abigail's heart? Find out in:

IN BED WITH THE OPPOSITION

Available December wherever books are sold.

Harlequin®

SPECIAL EDITION

Life, Love and Family

Karen Templeton

introduces

The FORTUNES *of* TEXAS: Whirlwind Romance

When a tornado destroys Red Rock, Texas, Christina Hastings finds herself trapped in the rubble with telecommunications heir Scott Fortune. He's handsome, smart and everything Christina has learned to guard herself against. As they await rescue, an unlikely attraction forms between the two and Scott soon finds himself wanting to know about this mysterious beauty. But can he catch Christina before she runs away from her true feelings?

FORTUNE'S CINDERELLA

Available December 27th wherever books are sold!